W9-AZU-715

Alvin Fernald,
Superweasel

Books for Young Readers
by Clifford B. Hicks

Fiction

ALVIN FERNALD, SUPERWEASEL

ALVIN FERNALD, MAYOR FOR A DAY

ALVIN FERNALD, FOREIGN TRADER

ALVIN'S SECRET CODE

THE MARVELOUS INVENTIONS OF ALVIN FERNALD

FIRST BOY ON THE MOON

Nonfiction

THE WORLD ABOVE

Weekly Reader Children's Book Club presents

Alvin Fernald,
Superweasel

by Clifford B. Hicks
illustrated by Bill Sokol

Holt, Rinehart and Winston
New York   Chicago   San Francisco

Library of Congress Cataloging in Publication Data
Hicks, Clifford B.
Alvin Fernald, superweasel.
SUMMARY: Alvin's pollution project is geared to
expose the biggest polluter in town—the owner of the
chemical plant.
[1. Pollution—Fiction] I. Sokol, Bill, illus.
II. Title.
PZ7.H5316Aks   [Fic]   73-21828
ISBN 0-03-012326-7

Printed in the United States of America: 074

for Melissa,
and all who come after

Alvin Fernald,
Superweasel

1. The Assignment

Alvin Fernald slumped at his desk as Miss Miles droned on. He was amusing himself with a silent mental exercise. His opponent was his own Magnificent Brain.

"Seat four, row two," Alvin whispered silently to himself.

"Room 201," responded his Magnificent Brain just as silently.

The whole idea of the game was to describe, in graduated steps, *where* the players were while they were playing the game.

"Roosevelt School," said Alvin.

"Town of Riverton."

"Melrose County."

"State of Indiana."

"North Central States." Alvin was proud of that one. He'd never thought of it before.

"United States of America."

"North American Continent."

"Northern Hemisphere." Ah! There was another new one, this time scored by the Magnificent Brain.

"Planet Earth."

"Solar system!" shot back the Magnificent Brain, believing it had won the contest.

"UNIVERSE!" Alvin banged his feet on the floor and shouted it aloud.

"Alvin!" The voice came from the general direction of Miss Miles's desk. "Alvin, please return from outer space by the first available rocketship and help us solve the serious problems we have here on Earth."

Alvin sat up straight. "What problems, Miss Miles?" he asked weakly.

"During your absence, the rest of the class has been discussing the pollution of our environment. I assume you know what pollution means, Alvin?"

"Yes'm. It means dirt."

Oliver Biggs, better known to the kids as Big Wind, or just plain Windy, snorted. Promptly the rest of the class giggled. Miss Miles turned to Windy, who was seated just in front of Alvin.

"Oliver, please explain to Alvin what pollution is."

"Pollution," said Windy in his superior voice, turning to look at Alvin, "is the contamination of our environment—land, water or air—with any foreign substance. Anything from a bubble-gum wrapper to a deadly poison can be a pollutant. Even unnecessary noise is considered a pollutant. In general, however, pollutants are usually defined as toxic substances."

Windy always uses big words to impress everybody, thought Alvin. *Well, he doesn't impress me.* Miss Miles was writing the word "pollution" on the blackboard and couldn't see him, so Alvin bonked Windy

2

on the head. The class laughed. Miss Miles whirled around.

"This subject is no joke," she said. "It is a deadly serious matter. We are poisoning our planet, and doing it very rapidly."

Miss Miles glanced at some notes on her desk. "Let me give you just one true illustration. A few years ago two men entered a bank in London, drew pistols, and escaped with the British equivalent of $22,000 in cash. They couldn't be recognized because they were wearing masks before they entered the door. And their disguises were perfect *because everyone else in London was wearing a mask, or had a scarf tied over his nose and mouth.*"

Alvin whistled. Miss Miles now had his attention. "Was it Halloween?" he asked.

"No. But at the time of the robbery, London was choking under a blanket of heavy smog. The people had been warned to wear masks because four thousand persons had died in a similar smog not long before."

"But that can't happen here," Theresa Undermine stated flatly. "Riverton isn't a big city like London."

"In the first place, we should all be concerned about everyone else on our planet," said Miss Miles sharply, "whether they live in our own town or not. In any case, Theresa, we *do* have lots of pollution right here in Riverton. The soil all over town is being polluted with chemicals that we ourselves spread, mainly to kill weeds and insects. And not only the soil is affected. According to last night's paper, our water rates

3

in Riverton are going up because the water is so impure it is taking more treatment to purify it."

"What can we do about that?" asked Alvin, mentally seeing a smog-mask covering his Magnificent Brain.

"There are several things you can do about it, Alvin. I really believe that it will be the children of the world who will clean up our environment—if anyone does." She paused. "As a matter of fact, that's the subject of our next assignment."

"I suppose you want us to write some dumb old theme on pollution," said Shoie. Shoie, whose real name was Wilfred Shoemaker, had been Alvin's closest friend for a zillion years. He was lousy at writing themes, but he was the Mightiest Athlete of Roosevelt School.

"No. No themes, Wilfred. But I *am* going to give you an assignment. You'll have a great deal of freedom to do it in your own way. And you'll have until the end of the school year to finish it."

Alvin groaned. Obviously the class was in for a lot of work.

"What's the assignment, Miss Miles?" asked Windy Biggs. "I can hardly wait to get to work on such an important subject." Windy was always trying to score points with the teacher.

" 'Hardly wait to get to work,' " mocked Alvin in a whisper.

Windy glared at him, and the class giggled.

"That will be enough, Alvin," Miss Miles said severely. She stood up. "This *is* a very important as-

4

signment, class. I'm assigning each of you, personally, to *do* something good for our environment—either to help clean it up, or to cut down the rate of pollution. Your project can deal with the pollution of the air, the soil, the water—any factor of our environment. And you can do anything you wish—*anything at all*—" she repeated the words slowly to emphasize them, "but at the end of the school year you will be called on to give an oral report on how you spent your time. That gives you two months to work on your project."

"Can two or three of us work together?" asked Theresa. She was smiling hungrily at Shoie, whom she adored. *She looks like one of those women vampires on the Saturday night horror show,* thought Alvin.

"Yes. You can join together for your project. But you will be asked for individual reports."

"I already know what I'm going to do," Windy announced. He always seemed to be one step ahead of everyone else in the class. "I'm going door to door and ask Riverton housewives to use nonpolluting detergents. Cleansing materials are among our biggest offenders."

"Why do you use such big words?" whispered Alvin. Then, more loudly, "You sound like you ate the dictionary for lunch."

Worm Wormley, who was sitting across the aisle, started laughing.

Windy ignored Alvin. "I'll ask my father to print some information on the subject that I can leave behind in each home." Mr. Biggs, Windy's father, was owner of the chemical plant out on Thompson Road.

He was also one of the richest men in town. All the kids knew this because Windy kept telling them so.

Theresa was still looking eagerly at Shoie. "Maybe two or three of us could clean up all the trash from the banks of the Weasel River," she said. The little river ran right through the center of town. It *did* seem to attract litter.

"I'm going to p-p-p-post No Littering signs in the p-p-park," said Worm Wormley, stuttering as he always did when he was excited. "And I'll get some empty oil drums from the oil company and put them around so p-p-people won't dump their trash all over the g-g-g-g-g-g—," he paused and swallowed, "—our environment."

"Maybe I'll plant trees," said Speedy Glomitz thoughtfully. "Trees help clean up the air," he added in explanation.

"I'm going to set up a recycling center," said The New Kid in Town. Nobody except the teacher ever called him anything but "The New Kid" even though he'd moved to Riverton more than two years before.

"What's a recycling center?" asked Alvin.

"Everyone knows that," said Windy in his superior way, just as The New Kid opened his mouth. "A recycling center is a collection point where you take all your old bottles and cans. They sort them, and turn them in for reprocessing into new bottles and cans, so they won't clutter up our environment."

Now the ideas came spontaneously from all over the room.

"I'm going to visit every single house in town," said

Doug Freeland, "and persuade everybody not to burn old trash or leaves. That will keep the air over Riverton a lot cleaner."

"Hey, Alvin," said Theresa, "what are you going to do?"

Alvin had been asking his Magnificent Brain that same question for ten minutes. Alvin always thought of his Magnificent Brain as something outside himself —as some other person. It was Shoie who had given that "other person" a name—the Magnificent Brain— because it came up with such stupendously crazy ideas. Frequently those ideas got Alvin in trouble, making him the best-known kid in Riverton, even if a lot of adults were a little leery of him. Old Mr. Fitz always crossed the street when he saw Alvin approaching.

"Just wait," said Alvin. "I've got a great idea. You'll see."

"I bet you don't have any idea at all," said Windy jeeringly.

"You wait. Just wait. I'll have the best antipollution project you ever heard of." He knew his voice sounded a bit desperate. "I'll do more to clean up Riverton than all the rest of you put together. You just wait. You'll see!"

But the Magnificent Brain was still a blank. Alvin just couldn't seem to energize the right circuits.

Alvin Fernald and his friend Shoie took the long way home from school, through the city park. The Weasel River ran right through the park, and they

bill sokol

scrambled down the bank of the little stream to look for the first crawdads of the year. The late-March sun was shining brightly in a cloudless sky, but there was a black, black cloud hanging over Alvin's head.

"It *does* look kind of scummy," said Shoie, pointing to the little river.

"Yeah. And look at all the trash along the bank."

There was a long pause. Alvin listlessly picked up a tin can and threw it into the muddy water. He was a short, slim boy with orange hair, and more freckles on one side of his face than the other.

"What's the matter, Alvin?" asked Shoie.

"I lied in school. I don't really have a pollution project."

"I figured that. I think Miss Miles knew it, too." Another pause. Then Shoie said, with no enthusiasm, "Hi, Windy."

Alvin looked upstream. Windy was kneeling beside the river, peering down into the water.

"Hi, Shoie," Windy said, ignoring Alvin completely.

"Whatcha' doing?" asked Shoie.

"Looking for oil on the surface. That's another form of environmental pollution."

"'Environmental pollution,'" mimicked Alvin. "Hey, why do you use all those big words? Nobody's impressed, you know."

Windy's face turned red. "You'd better watch what you say, Alvin Fernald. And you'd better not thump me on the head anymore, either."

"Or what?" Alvin picked up an old chunk of concrete and prepared to heave it into the water.

9

"Well. . . . Well. . . . Well, I'll get even. I might tell my dad. I'm warning you. Just watch out."

"*You're* warning *me*?" said Alvin as he threw the concrete. Suddenly he had a sense of impending disaster as his foot slipped in the mud at the edge of the water. Flailing his arms wildly, he tried to fling himself back to safety. One arm whipped around in a great half-circle, and he felt the shock in his fingers as his fist smacked Windy squarely on the chest. Windy's body flipped over in a full somersault, and he suddenly disappeared in the muddy water.

"Hey! What are you doing, Alvin?" shouted Shoie.

"I didn't mean to do it! I slipped!" Alvin reached out a hand to help Windy, but it was ignored.

"You—you—you're a nasty kid," sputtered Windy. Muddy water ran down his face, and his yellow shirt had turned a deep brown. He climbed out, slipping and sliding through the ooze.

"Honest, Windy! I didn't do it on purpose! I just slipped." Alvin *knew* he was telling the truth, but he also knew he never could persuade Windy that it was the truth. *"Honest!"*

"I'll get even with you, Alvin Fernald!" Windy sputtered as he scrambled up the bank. "You just wait. I'll tell my father, and he'll get even with you."

The last words were shouted.

Then there was a sudden and ominous silence as Windy climbed the riverbank and disappeared over the crest.

2. Birth of a Superhero

Shoie followed Alvin upstairs. Alvin automatically ducked his head as he opened the door to his room, but Shoie forgot all about the Foolproof Burglar Alarm that Alvin had invented. As the door swung open, a big boxing glove, strapped to the end of a heavy board, shot out and smacked Shoie across the side of the face.

"Doggone it, Alvin!" shouted Shoie, staggering around the room. "Why don't you disconnect that thing?"

"Then how would I keep out burglars?" Alvin slipped out of his school pants and put on a pair of jeans. On his inventing bench he spotted one-half of a peanut butter sandwich left over from the previous afternoon. Carefully judging the size of it, he put his finger on the exact center point, and ate the sandwich up to his fingernail. He handed the remainder to Shoie. Then he lay down on his bed and began to laugh.

"What's so funny?" mumbled Shoie through the stale sandwich.

"I was just thinking about how Windy Biggs looked when he climbed out of the river."

"I wouldn't be laughing if I were you. He really was mad. He's sure to tell his old man. Then there'll be a call to the police station, and the chief will call in your father and tell him." Alvin's father was a sergeant on the Riverton Police Force.

"Maybe. Honest, Shoie, I didn't push him on purpose. It was an accident."

"Talk about pollution," said Shoie. "Windy was covered with it. Remember how he tried to wipe that slimy stuff out of his eyes?"

Alvin rolled over on his side, facing Shoie. "Yeah. And that reminds me. What are we going to do for our antipollution project?"

"I dunno. Check that question through the Magnificent Brain, and see what comes out."

Alvin closed his eyes and pulled on his right ear. A moment later he said, "Cars cause lots of pollution. We could stuff a potato up every tail pipe that is spreading smoke."

Shoie carefully considered the idea. He had learned long ago not to immediately reject any idea, no matter how wild, that came from the M.B. Finally he said, "N-o-o-o. I don't think so. Too expensive. All those potatoes would cost a lot of money."

Alvin pulled his ear again. "We could sponsor an antipollution dance to raise the money to buy the potatoes to stick in the tail pipes. I'll bet we could even get the Grubby Toenails to play." The Grubby Toenails was a high school rock group.

"Get off that kick, Alvin. Try running the whole thing through the computer again."

Alvin squeezed his eyes shut and covered his right ear with his hand. As if it was a prearranged signal, the door flew open and a lithe little figure ducked under the boxing glove. The door slammed shut.

"Hi, Alvin. Hi, Shoie. What're we going to do this afternoon?"

"Get out, Pest," said Alvin ominously.

Alvin always called Daphne, his little sister, the Pest. As usual, she was dressed in Alvin's outgrown jeans, and her halo of straw-colored hair flowed down around her shoulders. She worshipped Alvin and, with or without his permission, she followed him wherever he went.

"Got any good ideas for antipollution projects?" asked Shoie. He always showed great respect for the Pest because in the past, she had rescued him (and Alvin, too) from some particularly wild situations brought on by ideas that poured from the M.B.

"Pollution. That means dirty stuff." She pushed her hair back across her shoulders and out of her eyes. "You could write poems about pollution and have them printed in the school paper."

Shoie snorted at the idea. Alvin asked jeeringly, "What do you know about writing poems?"

"Lots. We studied them in school today. We found out that some kids can't write poems at all, and I write them very easily."

"You're crazy," said Alvin to his little sister. "Let's see you write a poem about pollution."

13

She gazed out the window for a minute, then took a deep breath, closed her eyes, danced around in a complete circle, and said rapidly:

> Roses are red,
>   Violets are blue;
>   But who can see them?
>   Smog ruined the view.

"Hey! That's not bad," said Shoie.

"Try another," encouraged Alvin.

This time she gazed out of the window much longer. Her eyes glazed over. Suddenly she whirled about on one foot, and declared loudly:

> Drive on, drive on! In a traffic snarl,
>   We'll gas ourselves to death;
>   The fleas will dance upon our graves
>   If they can draw a breath.

"Hey, Pest, you really *can* write poetry," exclaimed Alvin. He considered for a moment. "But I'm no good as a poet, and if *you* wrote the antipollution poetry then it wouldn't be *my* project."

"Not your project." The Pest had a habit of repeating the words of other people, like a faint little echo.

"We've got to come up with something," said Alvin. "Now let's analyze the problem scientifically." That was one of his favorite sentences. "What does Miss Miles really want us to do?"

"Clean up our environment," said Shoie.

"But you can't do that all by yourselves," objected the Pest. "You'd need lots of people."

14

"Right," said Alvin. "So the best thing we can do is get *everybody* involved. We've got to figure out *who* the biggest polluters are around Riverton, and point them out to everybody in town. We'll put the glare of publicity on them!" He was warming to his subject.

"Right on!" declared Shoie enthusiastically.

The Pest whirled around, stopped abruptly, and proclaimed:

> *Stop DDT, and 2,4-D*
> *And all that poison junk;*
> *Stop ruining our 'vironment,*
> *A POLLUTER IS A PUNK!*

The Pest was one of the third-grade cheerleaders, so she shouted the last line.

"I already know who's the biggest polluter in town," announced Alvin quietly.

"Who?" asked Shoie.

"Think about it for a minute, old man. Remember when we used to be able to catch fish in Three Oaks Pond any time we hiked out there? Now there's not a single fish left alive in that pond. They're all dead, *killed by pollution.*"

"Who's polluting the pond?" asked Shoie indignantly.

"Well, we all know that the Weasel River runs into the *north* end of the pond, and then comes out again at the *south* end. Right? The river is bringing pollution into that pond."

"Where from?" asked the Pest.

"Shoie, do you remember that day last summer

15

when we hiked up the river to the chemical plant? When we got there, we discovered that a lot of oily, yellow stuff was pouring out of a pipe line from the plant, and running right into the river. That's the polluter—the chemical plant. Nature probably has been building that river and Three Oaks Pond for millions of years, and some lousy polluter destroys them in a year or two."

"Windy Biggs's old man owns the chemical plant," said Shoie softly. "*He's* the lousy polluter."

"Even if you know the chemical plant is spreading poison," said the Pest, "what can you do about it? Alvin, you're full of ideas, but how can a thirteen-year-old boy fight a big company like that? It would take Superman to accomplish anything."

Something clicked in the Magnificent Brain. He squeezed his eyes shut and thought for a long moment. Superman! "That's it!" he said triumphantly, sitting up on the edge of the bed. "That's what we'll do! That's our antipollution project!"

"Our antipollution project!" echoed the Pest.

"*What's* our antipollution project?" Shoie was baffled.

"Superman and Batman and Spiderman and all those other guys are *crime fighters*. We'll be crime fighters, too. We'll fight the greatest criminals of all—the *polluters*. On the blackest of nights we'll suddenly appear out of nowhere and strike back at them. We'll leave our secret mark behind. Then we'll disappear, as though we'd never existed! We'll be *superheroes!*" Alvin was getting carried away.

16

"Sounds like fun," said Shoie, not knowing exactly what Alvin had in mind. "What do we call ourselves?"

"Ah! That's very important." Alvin began pacing the floor. "If we want to strike hard at the polluters—focus publicity on them—then we strike, not as *three* persons, but as *one*. A single caped crusader who seems to be everywhere at once in his eternal battle against the arch fiends of pollution!"

"Oh, Alvin!" said the Pest. "You use such shivery words." She gazed admiringly at her brother. "Besides, you're including me in your project, too."

Alvin hadn't even thought about that. He'd included her subconsciously. "Well," he said gruffly, "you can come along and write poems."

"I still want to know *who* we're going to be," said Shoie.

"It should be some *living thing* out of nature, to represent our environment."

"A living thing out of nature," repeated the Pest. "Maybe an animal?"

"Right on!" encouraged Shoie. "Some brave animal—a real fighter."

"I have it!" exclaimed Alvin.

"What?" Shoie and the Pest asked simultaneously.

"We'll be The Weasel!" A pause. Then, "Even better, we'll be *Superweasel!*"

"Superweasel?"

"Sure. Grandpa Ketch told me all about weasels when I stayed at his farm last summer. Weasels are great. Pest, go get the 'W' volume of the encyclopedia."

17

bill sokol

The Pest skipped back a moment later with the book, easily ducking under the Foolproof Burglar Alarm. The three kids sat side by side on the edge of the bed. The Pest found the right page.

Across the top of the page was a picture showing a long, slender animal with a pointed nose. It was gracefully built, and looked particularly alert and intelligent.

" 'In its tireless destruction of vermin, rats and mice, the weasel is a friend of nature and of man,' " read Alvin.

" 'Friend of nature and of man.' "

" 'It is not so helpful, however, when it robs poultry houses,' " continued Alvin.

"We won't rob any poultry houses, will we?" asked the Pest. "I'm scared of live chickens."

"Of course not."

"It says here," said Shoie, reading ahead, "that the weasel is absolutely fearless."

"That's us," said Alvin.

" 'One species is called the ermine,' " quoted the Pest. " 'The fur is so magnificent that only royalty, in days gone by, was allowed to wear it.' Oh, Alvin, that's so romantic!"

"Fearless!" exclaimed Alvin. "A friend of nature and of man. That's us! Besides, we're trying to clean up the Weasel River, aren't we? So what could be better than Superweasel?" He paused, then dropped his voice until it was scarcely more than a whisper. "Superweasel! That name will be whispered in awe and admiration in thousands of homes—and cursed by polluters throughout the world." He sprang to his feet. "Follow me!" he shouted.

In the bathroom, Alvin opened the medicine cabinet and took out the bottle of iodine. "Hold your fingers over the sink," he directed.

The kids thrust their forefingers out, and Alvin placed a drop of iodine on each, including his own. "This is the way the Indians, who also were great pollution fighters, swore themselves to secrecy," he said solemnly. "They cut themselves, and then mixed their blood together." He coughed slightly. "I don't want the Pest to hurt herself, so we'll use iodine instead of blood. Now, do you solemnly swear to keep secret the identity of Superweasel?"

Simultaneously they said, "Yes!" Upon signal from Alvin they rubbed their red-smeared forefingers together.

"Superweasel," proclaimed Alvin in his deepest and most mysterious voice, "soon will strike terror into the hearts of criminal polluters all over the world."

The Pest whirled once on one foot, then said in her soft little voice:

> *Hurray, hurray, the Weasel's here!*
> *He saves our air and water!*
> *He does a job he needs to do—*
> *As 'portant as bread and botter!*

"Botter?" asked Shoie.

The Pest smiled sweetly up at him. "Otherwise it wouldn't rhyme."

3. The First Superadventure

"Hic!"

Alvin had the hiccups. Normally this was no problem (occasionally he faked the hiccups in school, just
to bug Miss Miles). But it isn't easy to sneak through
the darkness as a superbeing when you have the hiccups.

"Hic!"

"Doggone it, Alvin," whispered Shoie, "can't you be
quiet?"

"Be quiet," echoed the Pest.

Alvin turned off his flashlight, and stopped for a
moment to catch his breath. Just below him he could
hear the gurgle of the Weasel River as it rounded the
bend toward town. He looked up at the sky. There
was only a sliver of moon showing. Good. The darker
the better. Superweasel—consisting of three shadowy
figures—was at work on his first big assignment to
save the environment.

Alvin reached out and squeezed his sister's thin
little shoulder. "How about it, Pest?" he whispered.
"Do you feel like a guardian of the environment?"

"I feel like a cookie," she whispered. "It's been a long time since dinner."

And it *had* been a long time since they'd eaten. As a matter of fact, Alvin and the Pest were supposed to be in bed.

They'd gone to bed at their regular time, then waited until their parents were watching television. When they thought the coast was clear, Alvin activated his Portable Fire Escape (an old rope with knots in it, tied to the foot of his bed, and thrown out the window). As quietly as possible he and the Pest lowered themselves to the bushes outside the kitchen. They picked up an old, dented bucket from the garage, and headed down the dark streets.

Shoie was sitting under a streetlight on the corner of Maple and Third, waiting for them. "Power to Superweasel," he said, holding out his fist with his thumb straight up. Alvin grabbed the thumb in his fist, and the Pest grabbed Alvin's thumb. It was Superweasel's secret password and handshake.

"If I'm going to lead the way," Alvin said importantly, "then you carry the bucket, old bean."

"Okay." Shoie glanced at the bucket as he took it. "Hey, I remember this one. It's the bucket you brought to school when Miss Miles let us raise that little rabbit in the classroom. We used it to carry water and food."

"Never mind about that. Let's get going."

Now, scrambling along the riverbank through the darkness, Alvin wasn't so sure they were doing the right thing. What if Mom or Dad decided to look in on them while they slept? What if Superweasel was arrested for trespassing?

"Are you guys sure you want to go ahead with this?" he whispered.

"I think it's exciting," said the Pest.

"I'm okay," said Shoie, though his voice sounded doubtful. "How about you?"

"Hic!" Alvin turned on his flashlight and resumed his scrambling journey along the faint trail through the trees beside the stream.

Ten minutes later the kids came to a large clearing. Far out in the center they could see the chemical plant. Huge floodlights bathed it in the brillance of daylight. A high fence of mesh wire surrounded the plant. The little river ran along one side of the factory, just outside the fence.

"No *hic* flashlight from here on," declared Alvin. "We sneak up the riverbed until we're right beside the corner of the factory. That's where they're dumping the bad stuff into the river. There'll be at least one night watchman around, maybe more, so keep your heads down."

Alvin took a deep breath. Crouching low, he ran up the riverbank toward the factory. The other kids followed. Halfway to the fence, the bank dropped almost to water level, and they stumbled into a pool of light from the floodlamps. Alvin felt as though he were on some gigantic, brilliantly lighted stage. The riverbed made a big curve up ahead, and he figured they could save time by taking a shortcut across the clearing, then dropping back into the riverbed. Crouching even lower, he scurried across the clearing. Almost immediately he lost his balance and fell on his face in the wet grass. Shoie tripped over him, did a somersault in midair, and landed on his back.

"Harrrrrffffffff!" The bucket clanged across the ground.

"What's wrong with you guys?" whispered the Pest. "Can't you be quiet?"

Alvin scuttled on across to the stream bed, lowered himself down the bank, and found that once more he was in dark shadows. Two other figures came slithering down the bank.

"Ooooooooofff!" Instantly the Pest started scrambling right back up the bank, her head bathed in the factory's floodlights, her golden hair glistening. She was holding one hand over her nose and mouth, and seemed to be trying to escape.

Shoie, too, was gasping for breath. Alvin knew why. The awful odor went down his throat, through his lungs, and right on down to his toenails. "Hic!" The effect of the hiccup drew a new batch of the horrible stuff into his lungs. For a moment he thought he would pass out.

He jerked the Pest down beside him so she couldn't be seen from the factory, and risked turning on the flashlight.

At their feet, overgrown with weeds, was the mouth of a pipe about two feet in diameter. No one would ever find it—unless he followed his nose.

Alvin was turning purple, and risked one quick gasp to keep himself alive. He heard the sound of falling water, and aimed the beam of the flashlight at the liquid flowing in a steady stream from the pipe into Weasel River. It was a horrible dirty yellow color. Here was the source of the awful smell.

Alvin jerked the bucket out of Shoie's grasp and, hanging onto Shoie's jacket, he leaned way over and held the bucket under the lip of the pipe. Quickly it grew heavier. When he judged that the bucket was three-quarters full, he pulled himself erect and scrambled up the bank. He lay flat in the grass, but in full view of the factory.

Shoie and the Pest staggered up and dropped beside him. All three gulped the fresh air.

"Hic!" Alvin thrust the bucket as far as he could from his head.

"No wonder all the fish in Three Oaks Pond are dead," whispered Shoie.

"That's awful stuff!" said the Pest.

Alvin silently agreed with them, but didn't think they should discuss the subject here in the open. He put his fingers to his lips, and lifted his head to survey the situation. The entire fence, as far as he could see, was brightly lighted. But no. There was one exception. The factory's tall smokestack cast a dense shadow across one small section of the fence.

That shadow was where Superweasel must make his entry!

Alvin pushed himself to his feet, grabbed the bucket and, crouching low, ran for the fence. He hoped no watchman was looking in his direction. As he ran, the water sloshed out of the bucket and splashed across his pants legs and shoes. It was a horrible feeling, and smelled like he had stepped into a nest of dead skunks.

Alvin fully expected someone to shout at him at any moment. Although Shoie had started well behind him, the Mighty Athlete passed him in a burst of speed that made Alvin feel like he was crawling.

Superweasel—all three parts of him—aimed at the base of the fence. In the dim light Alvin could see that the bucket was still half-full of the poisonous liquid.

"Where's the clothesline?" he whispered.

The Pest unzipped her jacket. Coiled around her waist were about ten turns of her mother's best clothesline. Patiently she uncoiled it, then handed one end to Alvin and the other to Shoie. Alvin tied his end to the handle of the bucket.

"You get the honor, old bean," he whispered to Shoie. "You've always been the Mighty Athlete."

"Geeeeez! Thanks a lot. You guys can run if anything happens, but I'll be caught up there."

"Power to Superweasel!" said Alvin.

Shoie took a deep breath, then grabbed the end of the clothesline in his teeth. He shot up the fence like a monkey.

Alvin could barely see Shoie straddling the top of the fence, but he felt a sudden tug on the rope. He eased the bucket off the ground, and it disappeared into the darkness above.

"You next," ordered Alvin. "I want to be sure you can make it, so you won't be stuck out here all alone."

Actually (as Alvin well knew) the Pest was much

more athletic than he was. Inserting the tips of her little sneakers into the wire mesh, she moved rapidly upward. Alvin followed, wheezing.

The three figures straddled the top of the fence for a moment, staring out across the factory yard.

"Hic!"

"Can't you stop that, Alvin?" whispered the Pest. "Cathy Kemp says that if you cross your legs and your arms, lean as far backward as you can, hold your breath, and think about zebras it's a sure way—"

"Shusssssssh!" The sound was urgent. In the dim light, Alvin pointed. A man had just come around the corner of the building, and was walking slowly toward the fence. In his hand was a flashlight.

Alvin imagined that there was a gigantic gun strapped to the man's waist. He could feel the sweat pouring down his face in the cool night air.

The guard stopped directly beneath the three figures perched atop the fence.

"Hic!"

4. Superweasel Strikes!

The guard stopped abruptly; his figure froze.

Alvin was looking directly down at the top of the man's cap. The flashlight came on and swept around in a big circle. Even after it winked off Alvin could still see the man clearly. Would he look up? Time stood still—and so did four human figures, one on the ground and three directly above.

Finally the guard pushed his cap to the back of his head, scratched his forehead, and seemed to relax. He whistled softly to himself. At last he sauntered off toward the factory, and disappeared around the corner of the building.

"Hic!" Alvin almost exploded.

> *There's scum upon the water,*
>   *And we're here upon the fence;*
> *We'd be home in bed this minute*
>   *With an ounce of common sense.*

"Quiet!" ordered Alvin. "Poems aren't funny right now. We've got to get down from here. After I climb down inside the fence, you lower the bucket to me, Shoie. Then Superweasel will go to work."

His heart still pounding from their close call, Alvin climbed down the fence and dropped to the ground. Almost instantly the bucket came sailing down and hit him on the head. The thick liquid sloshed out, and he felt big drops of it running down inside his shirt.

"Gaaaaaarrrrg!" He could hardly breathe. He grabbed the rope and lowered the bucket to the ground.

Shoie and the Pest dropped to the ground beside him. Quickly Shoie untied the rope, and the Pest coiled it around her slim body again.

Alvin took a deep breath to clear the fumes from his head. Despite their close call, he was surprised they had conquered the fence so easily. On the ground, still in the shadow of the chimney, Alvin motioned to the others to follow, then crept over to the building. Cautiously he poked his head around the corner. There was the guard, now quite a distance away, sauntering toward the main gate.

Alvin had no way of knowing whether there were other watchmen in the plant, but Superweasel had to take a chance—now or never. Quickly he darted to a side door of the building. If the doors were all locked and required the watchman's keys, then all their work so far would be in vain.

He tried to push the door inward; it was as solid as a tomb. Turning the knob, he pulled it toward him, and uttered a soft sigh as the door swung outward.

The three kids darted in, and Alvin quickly swung the door shut behind them. Shoie was not quite through the door, and the edge of it struck the bucket. The liquid sloshed across Shoie's pants.

The awful odor, now so familiar, wafted up to their nostrils.

"Doggone it!" Shoie was angry. "I'm beginning to smell like a sewer!"

"Ugggggggh!" said the Pest.

"How'd you like to have that stuff poured down the back of your neck?" Alvin whispered. He risked switching on the flashlight. The bucket was a quarter-full of the dirty yellow stuff. He held his hand over the flashlight so only a tiny beam showed. "Follow me," he hissed.

They went up three steps, then crossed a large area with a fancy desk and switchboard at the end. A long hall stretched straight ahead, with doors on each side.

"I think we're in the offices," said Alvin.

"In the offices," echoed the Pest, her little voice high and scared.

They crept down the corridor, Shoie bringing up the rear with the bucket. At the end, they came to a pair of big glass doors. Beyond, they could hear water splashing. Alvin shined the beam of light on the doors. "Executive offices," he whispered, reading the fancy gold letters.

He pushed open one of the doors and went inside, stumbling over the thick carpeting. Again he risked shining the beam around the room. They were in another reception room, but here the furniture was the very finest; huge paintings hung on the walls. In the center of the room was a beautiful little statue, the miniature figure of a graceful woman pouring water from a jar. And it was real water that splashed down into the crystal-clear pool at her feet.

"Perfect!" exclaimed Alvin.

"What's perfect?" asked Shoie.

"The fountain. We'll dump the stuff into the pool."

"Won't it run right out the drain?" asked the Pest.

"No, Pest. This must be what they call a recirculating fountain. That means the water in the pool is pumped up through the statue, runs out through the lady's jar, back into the pool, and is pumped right back up again. The same water is used over and over."

"Over and over," repeated the Pest.

"Great!" whispered Shoie. "I can see what you mean."

Alvin took the bucket from Shoie, and handed him the flashlight. With the others watching, he poured every drop of the murky yellow stuff into the pool, turning the water yellow. Alvin began to gag. He held his breath as long as he could, then risked a deep breath. By now the polluted water was pouring in a steady stream from the jar the woman held in her hands, and the sharp smell was seeping through the room. Shoie flicked the beam of light into the woman's face. Alvin had the distinct impression that she was turning up her nose at the stench.

"Let's get out of here!" gasped Shoie.

"Out of here!"

"Wait!" said Alvin. He grabbed the flashlight and

31

handed Shoie the empty bucket. "Come with me." Alvin retreated from the pool to a desk at the corner of the room. Gulping in a few breaths of fresher air, he found a sheet of paper on top of the desk, along with a big felt-tip marker. Across the paper he scrawled:

SUPERWEASEL HAS STRUCK! THE SMELL
YOU SMELL IS THE POLUTION YOU ARE
DUMPING INTO WEASEL RIVER. BEWARE,
ALL CRIMINALS WHO POISEN OUR PLANET.
SUPERWEASEL WILL FIND YOU AND STRIKE
AGAIN!
SUPERWEASEL

"You never were a very good speller, Alvin," said the Pest critically.

Alvin found some tape on the desk and, holding his breath, walked over to the statue. He taped the sign to the lady's neck. For a moment he stepped back and surveyed his work. In his opinion the sign improved the lady; she certainly wasn't wearing many clothes. Then, coughing and sputtering, he retreated across the room.

At that moment he heard the creak of a door somewhere within the building. . . .

The kids froze.

Then Alvin Fernald sprang into action. He swept the flashlight around the room and spotted a door with "Randolph E. Biggs, President" lettered across it in fancy gold. "Follow me," he hissed. He opened the door and slipped inside. The Pest followed, then

Shoie, who banged the bucket against the door on the way through.

"Sssssshhh!" Alvin eased the door shut.

A moment later they heard the door to the outer office open, then a gasping cough.

"Good Lord!" a man's voice said.

Alvin could imagine the night watchman reading the sign on the statue. Suddenly there was movement on the other side of the door, the click of a phone picked up, the whirrrr of the dial.

"Hello, Mr. Biggs." Then a cough. "This is Berger, the watchman at the plant. Sorry to bother you this time of night, sir, but I thought you should know that something funny's going on here. . . ." The man sniffed, then coughed. . . . "Somebody's been in your outer office. I'm going to check your private office next. . . . Yes, sir. I'll meet you at the front gate."

Alvin heard the slam of the receiver, then the soft shuffle of footsteps in the thick carpet. The man was coming straight toward them!

He pulled the other kids flat against the wall. The door swung slowly open, with the kids behind it. There was a click, and the room suddenly was flooded with light. A long moment of silence, then the light clicked off and the door closed again.

"Hic!" Alvin clapped his hand over his mouth. Surely the guard had heard him. Then, with relief, he heard the outer door close. Shoie and the Pest stirred beside him. "Wait," he whispered.

Nerves on edge, he forced himself to count to one hundred by fives. Only then did he open the door. He

slipped across the reception room, and eased open the door to the hallway. At the far end a bobbing circle of light vanished as he watched. The guard had turned a corner of the corridor.

The three kids slipped like shadows down the hallway. At the far end, Alvin opened the door through which they had entered the building. The guard was still ahead of them, now hurrying across the paved area toward the front gate.

Alvin sprinted toward the fence where the shadow of the chimney cut across it. Halfway there, Shoie and the Pest passed him as though he was standing still.

The others were halfway up the wire mesh by the time he reached it. He was still breathing hard and struggling upward when Shoie spoke into the night air.

"Holy smoke!"

"What's the matter? Alvin clawed his way to the top, and all three figures momentarily hung there as though suspended in the middle of the night.

"I forgot the bucket! It's back in Mr. Biggs's office."

"Well of all the stupid—" Alvin let the sentence hang, his heart sinking. He knew that the bucket might eventually be traced to his house. His fingerprints were all over it, and so were Shoie's.

The Magnificent Brain suddenly flashed a picture of Alvin in prison serving a ninety-nine-year-term for breaking and entering, trespassing, damaging property, vandalism and a dozen other charges.

The purr of a powerful automobile engine shook

the picture from his mind. The front gate clanged open.

"We've got to get out of here!" said Alvin, starting to climb down the other side of the fence.

There was a shout from the direction of the front gate, then the clatter of footsteps on the pavement. Alvin dropped the last five feet to the ground and raced toward the river. Shoie and the Pest had already disappeared over the edge of the bank.

There was another shout behind him. Alvin was certain he'd been spotted. He expected to hear the sound of a gun at any moment. At last he tumbled into the relative safety of the creek bed. The odor here was as awful as ever, but he preferred it to poking his head back up into the night air.

Superweasel had struck—and probably had made a real mess of things in more ways than one!

5. A Strategy Meeting

There it was, in a big, bold headline:

MYSTERY BREAK-IN AT CHEMICAL PLANT

The three individual parts of Superweasel were again in Alvin's bedroom, seated side by side on the edge of the bed, pulling the afternoon paper this way and that. Finally the Pest said, "Go ahead, Alvin. You read it aloud."

Alvin cleared his throat as though he were about to make an important announcement, then began:

One or more persons, for reasons not yet known, broke into the Biggs Chemical plant last night, according to Police Chief Robert C. Eaton.

"Burglary was not the motive," Chief Eaton stated flatly. "Nothing was taken. The criminal was obviously very clever—much more resourceful than the average burglar. As yet we have not determined how he gained access to the plant. The Biggs factory is completely encircled by a high wire fence which is fully floodlighted at night. Anyone attempting to scale the

37

fence would have been seen by one of the night guards."

The criminal or criminals left three items of evidence behind:

1. A dented bucket of unknown origin. The police say this may provide fingerprints or other clues.

2. A particularly bad-smelling substance, dirty yellowish in color, which was poured into a small decorative fountain in the middle of the executive reception room. Police theorize that this substance was brought to the fountain inside the bucket. The substance had such a nauseating odor that the executive offices at the plant could not be used today.

3. A sign, draped around a statuette in the fountain, which read: SUPERWEASEL HAS STRUCK! THE SMELL YOU SMELL IS THE POLLUTION YOU ARE DUMPING INTO WEASEL RIVER. BEWARE, ALL CRIMINALS WHO POISON OUR PLANET. SUPERWEASEL WILL FIND YOU AND STRIKE AGAIN!

SUPERWEASEL.

"Look, Alvin," interrupted the Pest, her blue eyes shining with excitement, "they corrected your misspelled words."

Alvin ignored her, and went on reading:

When a reporter for the *Daily Bugle* contacted Randolph E. Biggs, owner and manager of the chemical plant, he stated that he had no idea why anyone would want to break into the plant, nor the nature of the mysterious substance dumped into the pool.

"It is obvious we are dealing with a sick mind,

indeed a criminal mind," said Mr. Biggs. "Anyone who would dump such a foul-smelling substance anywhere near other human beings is a vandal. I intend to prosecute this so-called 'Superweasel' to the very limit of the law.

"He probably is someone who is a nut on ecology," went on Mr. Biggs, "but there is not the slightest reason for him to declare private war on our company. We are proud of our efforts to protect Riverton's environment, and are extremely careful never to pollute the air, soil, or water."

"Hogwash!" exclaimed Shoie.

The Pest was so angry that she leaped to her feet and stuck her tongue out at the newspaper.

"Wait," said Alvin. "There's one more paragraph."

The *Daily Bugle*, with its private contacts, has made every effort to determine the identity of 'Superweasel,' but with no success. Anyone knowing his identity is urgently requested to call the City Desk of the *Bugle* immediately, in view of Superweasel's stated threat to strike again.

"You're doggone right Superweasel will strike again!" exclaimed Shoie. "We're not going to let that guy Biggs get away with all his sweet talk while he's ruining the river!"

"Ruining the river!" said the Pest.

"Calm down, you guys. Of *course* we're not going to let him get away with it, and of *course* Superweasel will strike again. The sooner the better. Actually, this news story is great. It's exactly what we needed to give Superweasel a rousing start in his battle against polluters. Now, everyone will be talking about Superweasel. Anything he does from now on will be big news."

"Well, what *are* we going to do?" asked Shoie.

Alvin ran the question through the Magnificent Brain. He was just beginning to get some results when the Pest suddenly tossed her hair, closed her eyes and recited:

> *The Weasel needs some super ways*
> *To fight the town's pollution;*
> *So try your best, you two nitwits*
> *To find the best solution.*

"That's awful," said Shoie.

"I never agreed with you more, old bean," said Alvin. "Besides, Pest, you threw the Magnificent Brain out of whack." He pulled on his ear. "Do either of you have any good ideas?"

There was a long pause, then Shoie said, "We could probably find some dead fish floating in the river down below the dam. Superweasel could do something with them."

"Not bad," said Alvin thoughtfully. "Not bad at all. The dead fish would *prove* that the chemical plant is killing wildlife. But what could we *do* with dead fish that would cause a lot of excitement—and get Superweasel some more attention?"

Another long pause. Then the Pest piped up. "We

could throw them into the secretarial pool," she offered.

Alvin started to laugh. "Pest," he gasped, "What do you know about the secretarial pool?"

"Well," she said, now embarrassed, "in school, we've been studying the different kinds of jobs, and all big companies have a secretarial pool. The secretaries swim in it . . ."

Alvin interrupted her. "That's a good one, oh, that's a prize! Pest, a secretarial pool is a group of secretaries. Whenever one of the bosses needs a secretary, he just calls the secretarial pool and asks for a secretary."

The Pest looked down at her sneakers. "Well. Well, it's not such a bad idea anyway. I'll bet if we tossed some dead fish in among all those secretaries we could cause a lot of excitement."

A thoughtful look crossed Alvin's face. "Speaking of pools," he said, "you may have a good idea, Pest. The Biggs family has the biggest swimming pool in town. And it's heated, so they are already using it. Maybe a few dead fish in his swimming pool would make Mr. Biggs admit what he's done to the fish in Weasel River and the pond."

"Great!" said Shoie.

"It's not a bad idea," said Alvin thoughtfully, "but not really a good one, either. Mr. Biggs probably would clean out the fish without saying anything, and no one would know that Superweasel had struck again. No, we need something even better." A pause.

41

"We've got to figure out some way to get Biggs to close up that sewer running into the river."

Shoie usually left the great ideas to Alvin, but suddenly he could hardly wait to talk. "I've got it! From what you just said, Alvin! Why don't *we* dam up that sewer?"

Alvin's eyes opened wide. He reached out and pounded Shoie on the back. "Old bean, I always knew you had a great brain, too. If we can dam up that drainpipe, then that lousy yellow stuff will back up until it begins to flood the factory grounds. And Biggs won't even realize what is happening until suddenly his whole factory will smell like the Weasel River. Do you suppose we can plug that pipe, and somehow let people know it was Superweasel who did it?"

"Superweasel can do anything," declared Shoie, proud of his idea.

"I still like the other idea—about the dead fish in Mr. Biggs's swimming pool," said the Pest stubbornly.

"Okay," announced Alvin. "Pest, you toss the dead fish in the swimming pool while Shoie and I are damming the sewer pipe. That way Superweasel will strike in two places at the same time. Agreed?"

"Right!" the other two said enthusiastically.

"Then we have some planning to do. Let's make a list of everything we need. Pest, hand me a pencil and paper off the desk. . . ."

His little sister didn't respond. She sat motionless, a faraway look in her eyes. Alvin bonked her on the head. "Wake up, Sis."

He hardly ever called her Sis. When he did, it was

to express a fondness for her that he didn't want to put into words.

"I have a great idea!" she said suddenly. "Oh, Alvin, it's so good I'm about to explode. It will help get Superweasel oodles of publicity."

"Well. What is it?"

"Oh, no. I'm not going to tell you now. I want to surprise you later."

"I suppose you're going to put on a diving exhibition in the secretarial pool," he kidded her.

But the Pest was far off. Far off in another world.

6. A Loud Rip in the Night

Again Superweasel sneaked out long after he was supposed to be in bed. This time the kids met in front of the pickle works on the west side of town, just a couple of blocks from the Biggs home.

It was a Saturday night, three days after their planning session. They'd been jittery all day, waiting for Superweasel's second adventure to begin.

Alvin and the Pest had arrived at the pickle works first. The Pest was carrying a large paper sack. Alvin had demanded to see what was in it, but she had refused.

Moments later Shoie appeared in the pool of light. In one hand he, too, carried a paper sack; in the other hand a short-handled shovel.

"Power to Superweasel!" whispered Shoie.

"Power to Superweasel."

"Do you have the fish?" asked Alvin.

Shoie opened the mouth of the sack. Alvin tried to look inside, but the light was too dim to see anything. He could smell it though. One whiff of the dead fish and he quickly closed the bag.

"Pfoooooooey!" he exclaimed, handing the sack to his sister. "Here they are, Pest." He stared at her for a moment. His voice took on a strange softness. "Sis, are you sure you'll be all right? I mean, I wouldn't want you to get hurt. Are you sure you can toss those fish into the Biggses' swimming pool without getting caught? And then get back home, and back into your room?"

"Power to Superweasel," said the Pest solemnly. "Don't worry, Alvin. I can do it. I won't let you guys down."

"Okay. Then this is where we split. You go on over to the Biggs house, and Shoie and I will head up the river just like we planned."

"Wait just a minute, Alvin," said the Pest, an edge of excitement in her voice. She held out the mysterious paper bag. "Your surprise. I only had time to make one of them. Maybe later I'll be able to make two more. Anyway, this one's for you, Alvin."

"What is it?" he asked, opening the bag.

"A Superweasel costume," she announced proudly. "Batman has a costume, and Superman has a costume, and Spiderman has a costume, so I made Superweasel a costume."

Alvin took it out and looked at it. "Not bad. If I'm seen, the newspaper will hear about it, and we'll get even more publicity. Let me try it on."

"Not under the streetlight," warned Shoie. "We'd better go around to the alley, where nobody will see us."

Alvin struggled into the costume. As the Pest

45

bill sokol

coached him, he slipped the knit legs of his long winter underwear over his jeans. The jeans created big lumps all over his legs and hips, but the Pest squished the lumps around until at least he was comfortable.

"Put on the shirt," the Pest whispered proudly.

Alvin slipped the old potato sack over his head, stuck his arms through two holes, and pulled the ragged hem of the homemade shirt down to his waist. Letters painted across his chest read SUPER-WEASEL.

"Here's your cape, Alvin," the Pest said. She draped the black velvet fabric, left over from her dancing costume, across his shoulders and tied it with a string at his throat. Then she reached in her bag and pulled out a mask.

"*Could* be a weasel mask at that," he said, slipping it down over his face.

Shoie had been watching in silence. Now he began to laugh, softly at first, then more loudly, finally roaring. He dropped to his knees and beat the ground with his fists. "Man, do you look weird!" he gasped.

"Sssh!" hissed Alvin. "Doggone it, Shoie, do you want everybody in town to see us? Come on. Let's get out of here."

They circled the building, back to the street. Shoie was still trying to control his laughter.

"Good luck, Sis," said Alvin softly. "Be careful."

"You too, Superweasel." She began to giggle. "You *do* look sort of funny, Alvin." She dashed off down the street.

Alvin and Shoie turned in the other direction. Superweasel was about to strike again.

Trying to negotiate the path along the river at night was tiring work, and they were exhausted when they finally approached the sewer pipe just outside the chemical plant. For the last hundred yards or so they didn't dare use Shoie's flashlight. Twice, in the darkness, Shoie fell into the river. Alvin had found Superweasel's mask unbearably hot, and had pushed it up on top of his head, where it grinned at the stars.

Now the discharge pipe was at their feet, hidden by the weeds. They stood beside it for a moment, listening. Had they been heard by the watchman inside the plant?

Alvin put his lips close to Shoie's ear. "Well, here goes. No use wasting time. Why don't you wade in after the rocks? That way I can keep my costume dry. I'll get any junk I can find along the bank, and also shovel in the dirt."

Shoie sighed. "Okay, old bean. I'm already wet." He waded out into the stream. Alvin placed the shovel where he could find it, and crawled along the bank of the stream, feeling for anything that might serve as material for a dam. He found an old board, a piece of a fence post, and a rusty square of sheet metal. He dragged these back to the pipe and lowered them across its mouth. Shoie promptly stacked three big rocks where they would hold the junk in place. Alvin picked up the shovel and scooped loose dirt and gravel across the stack of debris.

Every few minutes they *had* to stop and climb up to the top of the bank for fresh air. The odor coming from the pipe was sickening. But they kept working. And as they worked, the flow from the pipe became only a tiny trickle, and the odor diminished, too.

Alvin risked turning on the flashlight for one quick inspection of the dam. Only a few drops of yellow liquid now oozed across the dam, right at the top of the pipe, and Shoie quickly stopped even that small leak. They had stopped the flow of the awful stuff; soon it would fill the pipe.

"Quick!" whispered Alvin. "I'm starting Phase Two."

"Are you sure you want to? I mean, they've probably got extra guards in there now. Maybe you better not risk it."

"Give me the flag," Alvin demanded. Though he was feeling brave at the moment, he knew from long experience it was a feeling that wouldn't last. He'd better move fast.

Shoie located his paper bag where he had dropped it along the bank. He pulled out a folded piece of cloth. Alvin slipped it beneath his Superweasel shirt and stuffed it under his belt. For Phase Two he'd need both hands free.

"Good luck, old man," whispered Shoie.

Alvin nodded, then scrambled up the bank and crawled toward the spot in the factory fence that they had used so successfully a few nights before.

Halfway up the fence, Alvin begain feeling lonesome. The fence somehow seemed much higher tonight, and the light much brighter than it had been before. During their planning session they had decided, quite logically, that there was no reason for two of them to risk capture. Now he wished Shoie was along. In fact, Shoie *should* be doing this job. After all, wasn't he the Mighty Athlete?

Alvin had pulled the mask down over his face when he left the safety of the stream bed. As a result, he couldn't see very clearly in any direction except straight ahead. Twice, as he climbed, he had the distinct feeling that he was being watched, but he couldn't spot the watcher.

At the top of the fence Superweasel slipped one leg across, then the other, and was about to step downward when he discovered that he was stuck; he couldn't move. Frantically he clung to the fence with one hand and felt about him with the other, trying to find what had seized him. At last he found it. The bottom of his cape was twisted into a knot that was snagged on one of the sharp wires across the top of the fence.

He grabbed the cape and jerked with all the strength in his one arm. A loud ripping sound seemed to echo through the night. But he was free!

He climbed down inside the fence as fast as he could, hoping that he wasn't plopping right into the arms of a guard.

Just as he hit the ground he heard a shout, then the sound of feet running toward him.

7. Who Can Stop Superweasel?

Superweasel dashed frantically around the corner of the plant, looking about for a place to hide. There was no cover, just a lone car in the middle of the big parking lot. It probably belonged to one of the guards. He ran to it and opened the back door.

Suddenly the Magnificent Brain flashed a warning —and an idea—to him. Instead of climbing into the car, Alvin slammed the door as loudly as he could, then dived under the car.

None too soon. Feet pounded around the corner of the building, then stopped momentarily. A man's deep voice said softly, "He's inside my car!"

"Yeah!" said another voice. Then the sound of feet scuffling toward him.

The toes of a pair of polished boots appeared right in front of Alvin's nose. It was stifling inside the mask, and he could feel the sweat rolling down his face.

Suddenly the doors flew open on both sides of the car.

"Come out of there!" ordered the deep voice.

A pause. Then, "There's no one in there," said the other voice.

"Something funny is going on here. I *did* see a figure —looked like some kind of a big animal—run around the corner of the building. Didn't I? Didn't *you?* I'm not going off my rocker, am I George?"

"Naw. I saw the same thing. Do you suppose it could have been that Superweasel guy?"

"I'll bet that's who it was. He sure does know how to appear and disappear." The words were spoken with grudging admiration. "And we don't even know whether he's armed. We'd better be careful. Let's not run around out here in the open any more than we have to. We're sitting ducks because we don't know where *he* is. Tell you what. Get into my car, and I'll drop you at the phone by the front gate. You call Mr. Biggs and tell him I'm on my way over to pick him up. Tell him Superweasel is loose somewhere inside the plant. Maybe he'd better bring some help."

"Right."

The springs of the car squeaked as the two men climbed in. The engine roared into life, and the car squealed into motion. Alvin had moved his right hand just in time. Suddenly he found himself lying in full view, in the glare of the floodlights, his nose pressed against the concrete. He lay still until the car was well out of the way and he couldn't be seen in the rear-view mirror.

At that moment his nose detected something. It was the smell of the yellow liquid, faint now, but getting stronger every second.

Alvin raised his head. Oozing across the pavement toward him, out from under the back door of the factory, came a trickle of water. Except, as Alvin knew, it wasn't just water. It was poison—poison for fish, frogs, crawdads, everything that lived in the river.

Superweasel had succeeded in damming the pipe!

Alvin's courage was renewed. He leaped to his feet and ran to the building, cape flowing out behind. Peering around the corner, he saw the gate close behind the car, then the second guard walk to a phone booth beside the gate.

Alvin felt a prickle of excitement—and fear. Should he go ahead with his plan? Or should he give up, knowing he'd be detected if he stayed inside the fence much longer?

Superweasel!

The name popped through the circuits of the Magnificent Brain. He couldn't back out now. If the kids of the world were ever going to do anything to fight pollution, they'd have to use all the ingenuity and courage they possessed.

Alvin slipped around the corner and raced for the front door, in full view of the guard in the phone booth if he should turn his head. It seemed a million miles to the entryway, but he made it, and breathed a sigh of relief when he found the door unlocked. Inside, he suddenly felt much safer.

He cautiously peered back out through the big glass door. The guard had emerged from the phone booth, and now was standing beside it, sniffing the air. He looked suspiciously toward the corner of the building. It was apparent that he wanted to investigate the smell, yet was afraid to set out alone.

Alvin waited in agonized suspense. Perhaps he'd done the wrong thing. Now he was stuck in the building. There was no place else for him to go.

Headlights came boring through the night, and two cars pulled up in front of the fence. The guard opened the gate, let the cars through, and then locked it behind them. Alvin watched in terror as the two cars drove up and parked directly in front of him. He tried to move, to slip farther into the building, but seemed frozen to the spot.

Mr. Biggs and the guard climbed out of one car. From the other emerged Mr. Moser, star reporter of the *Daily Bugle,* his hand protecting the flash camera he always carried on a cord around his neck.

Now all four men were talking at the curb just outside. Alvin eased the door open an inch so he could hear.

"—bother you, Mr. Biggs," one of the guards was saying, "but there's something funny going on here. I think we have Superweasel trapped inside the fence." Alvin could hear the words clearly.

"Nonsense!" snapped Mr. Biggs. "This Superweasel—whoever he is—has just been at my home. I found several dead fish in my swimming pool, and a warning sign on my diving board. It was some kind of childish poem, and was signed 'Superweasel.' I called Mr. Moser here to show him the damage—the outright vandalism—this criminal trespasser is causing. He was there when your call came in. Now—" his voice became slightly sarcastic, "—suppose you tell me how Superweasel can be in two places at one time."

"I dunno, Mr. Biggs. I dunno anything about Superweasel. All I know is that I saw something that looked like a big animal run around the corner of the factory and disappear into thin air. And since then, there's been this horrible smell coming from somewhere at the back of the factory."

There was a pause as all noses began to sniff the air.

"You're right," said Mr. Biggs. "But I don't know why two healthy men, both armed, can't guard the inside of a high fence." He sniffed again. "Something *is* wrong, though. Let's take a look back there."

The four men headed toward the other side of the building, one guard on each side of Mr. Biggs, with Mr. Moser trailing behind, notebook sticking out of his pocket and his camera held ready in his hands.

The instant they disappeared, Alvin raced out the door toward the flagpole that stood smack in front of the building. As he ran, he tugged the piece of cloth from beneath his belt. He slid to a stop at the foot of the flagpole.

Ever since he'd been in first grade, he'd enjoyed helping Mr. Maloney raise the flag in front of the school, and now he was doing it himself. Only this flag was an old piece of sheet, with letters spray-painted across the front. Strings were tied at two of the corners, and Alvin now fumbled with one of them in his excitement. Finally he managed to tie it to the rope that ran up the flagpole, then fastened the other one, too. He pulled on the rope, and the homemade pennant sailed upward.

But it sailed upward with a horrible squeak of the pulleys, a shrill squeal that cut through the night.

Alvin was sure the sound could be heard all the way around the building. Frantically he pulled hand over hand on the rope until the homemade flag jolted to a stop at the top of the pole. He tied the rope to the pole, then raced back toward the front door.

He was just swinging open the door when one of the guards dashed around the corner of the building and spotted him. "Stop or I'll shoot!" he shouted, reaching for his gun.

Alvin dived inside and raced blindly down a corridor. He turned left down a hallway lighted by a single overhead bulb. At the end of the corridor he spotted a swinging door. As he ran toward it, he knew that the guards and Mr. Biggs could hear his footsteps and would follow him anywhere he went. He was certain to be caught.

But as always in Alvin's moments of desperation, the Magnificent Brain came through. Just as he reached the door, a sudden thought flashed through his mind. He gave the door a tremendous shove. Then he ducked into a nearby doorway.

He found himself in a janitor's closet filled with brooms, mops and cleaning supplies. Standing there in the dim light he could hear the slapping sound as the corridor door swung to and fro. At the same moment he heard what sounded like an army of footsteps racing toward him down the hallway.

"This way!" shouted one of the guards.

The door to the closet was wide open, and Alvin was perfectly visible had the men glanced in his direction. But they were too intent on slamming through the doorway and capturing him somewhere on the other side. He *did* notice a strange thing. Only three men raced past. Mr. Moser wasn't with them.

Alvin slipped back into the corridor, and retraced his steps as silently as he could. No one was in front of the building, so he raced out the front door, and around the corner, heading for the fence.

Abruptly he slid to a stop.

Not more than ten feet from him Mr. Moser was kneeling on the ground. His hand was feeling the wet pavement. By now the whole area behind the factory was wet. Mr. Moser raised his hand to his nose. His eyes came up to lock with Alvin's. Both figures remained motionless.

It was Mr. Moser who broke the silence. "Pfoo-ooooey! The stuff smells awful! No wonder you're trying to keep it out of the river."

Alvin tried to say something, but simply gurgled.

"Mr. Biggs was lying when he told me he wasn't causing any pollution. Right? He's been getting rid of this stuff by dumping it in our river. Right?"

Alvin nodded his head.

Mr. Moser looked Alvin up and down. "That's some get-up you're wearing, young feller. So you're Super-weasel!"

Alvin nodded again.

"Are you going to tell me who you really are?"

Alvin shook his head.

"Well, you'd better get out of here. Biggs and those guards will be coming out here any minute."

"Thanks!" Alvin croaked behind his mask.

"You can count on my help, Superweasel. You need publicity. Right? I'll give you plenty of publicity, as long as you *don't try any vandalism, any real destruction of anyone else's property*. You understand? *No vandalism!* Right?"

"No vandalism!" croaked Alvin over his shoulder as he ran for the fence.

The first flashbulb popped when he was halfway up the fence, and from then on they flashed just as fast as Mr. Moser could operate the camera. Superweasel threw himself over the top and was halfway down the other side when there was a shout from the direction of the factory. He glanced back to see the guards and Mr. Biggs running toward Mr. Moser.

Alvin had just dropped to the ground when he heard Mr. Biggs exclaim angrily, "Why didn't you stop him?"

"Who can stop Superweasel?" asked Mr. Moser quietly. "Now, Mr. Biggs, why don't you tell me about that smelly stuff that's flooding your factory grounds? You've been dumping it in the river. Right?"

Superweasel raced off into the night. His cape flowed regally out behind, and Alvin knew how Superman must feel during his adventures. It gave him a sense of superpower.

8. Victory—and a New Enemy

Three weary kids sneaked back into two houses—
but only after they had hidden the Superweasel costume and Shoie's smelly pants in the "clubhouse" they
had built from scrap lumber years before. The little
shed was out on the back corner of Shoie's lot; not
much smell should reach the house.

Sunday passed uneventfully. Monday, though,
brought new developments.

On Monday morning Alvin and Shoie, through no
fault of their own, got into trouble at school. Miss
Miles announced that she wanted a progress report
from each student on his—or her—antipollution project. Windy Biggs went to great lengths, and long
words, to explain his analysis of the chemicals in each
of the different detergents available to housewives.

I'll bet he didn't do a bit of that work, thought
Alvin. *I'll bet his dad had it done for him, at the
laboratory in the chemical plant.*

Worm Wormley stuttered out the fact that he had
posted No Littering signs in eighteen d-d-d-d-d-
separate spots around Riverton. And Speedy Glomitz

announced that so far he had planted six small trees donated to his project by Sally Barclay, whose husband ran the Riverton Nursery.

"What about you, Alvin?" asked Miss Miles.

He had dreaded the question. How could he say a word? He'd taken a blood oath—at least an iodine one—not to reveal anything about Superweasel.

"Well, Shoie and I are doing sort of a special kind of a project together."

Miss Miles seemed to be waiting for him to say more. At last she said, "Well, Alvin, what sort of a special kind of a project?"

"Well—well—we're trying to get people to—to stop polluting their environment."

"We're all trying to do that, Alvin. Just *how* are you doing it?"

"I'd rather not say just now, Miss Miles." He evaded her eyes, glancing around the room. He found himself staring at Windy Biggs. Windy had a strange look on his face.

"Alvin, I hope you and Wilfred are not just ignoring this assignment."

As they walked up the sidewalk, on their way to Alvin's room, Alvin noticed the afternoon paper on the front steps. "Wow! Look at that, old bean!" he exclaimed.

At least half the front page was covered with a huge picture of Superweasel scrambling up the fence, his masked face looking straight down at the camera. Alvin studied the picture for a moment, admiring how handsome he was as a caped crusader. Then he headed through the front door and up the stairs to his room. The Pest was already inside, holding the Foolproof Burglar Alarm so it wouldn't clobber Shoie.

"Doggone it!" Alvin said. "How did you get in here? I double-locked my room this morning."

"I have ways," she said with a smile.

Alvin was too excited to pursue the argument. He launched himself onto his bed, landed on his stomach, opened the paper flat on the bedspread, and propped his head in his hands.

"Read it aloud," said Shoie.

"Well, you can see the big headline from anywhere in the room. It says:

MYSTERY FIGURE
STARTS ANTIPOLLUTION WAR!

A strange masked figure calling himself Superweasel Saturday night launched an all-out fight on the environmental polluters of Riverton.

The unknown man, dressed in a humorous costume that looks like a cross between a weasel and Superman, dammed a sewage pipe belonging to the Biggs Chemical Company. Unknown to city and state environmental authorities, the pipe was discharging an extremely poisonous material into the Weasel River. On Saturday the dammed-up effluent backed up into the Biggs factory. As a result, the factory had to remain closed today because of the bad odor.

In a rare example of audacity, Superweasel invaded the locked Biggs plant and, despite armed guards, ran a homemade flag up the flagpole. Across the flag were printed the words *"Beware, polluters! Superweasel will strike again!"*

The person who calls himself Superweasel apparently has magic powers. At approximately the same time he was seen at the plant, several dead fish, poisoned by the chemical effluent, were tossed into a swimming pool on the estate of Mr. Randolph E. Biggs, owner and president of the plant. A sign was taped to the swimming pool gate reading:

Here are some fish, some poor dead fish—
You killed them with a smell;
You must be proud, you nasty man, . .
I hope you go to—jail.

The note was signed Superweasel.

Through a remarkable set of circumstances, this reporter had the opportunity to conduct a short interview with Superweasel as he was escaping from the locked plant. At that time he "swore vengeance on all polluters of our environment." He said that anyone he caught in any type of pollution would "suffer the same type of damage as that person was doing to the environment."

"Hey, old bean," said Shoie, with a big grin on his face. "You sure do spout the big words."

"That isn't exactly what I said. I think Mr. Moser is putting words in Superweasel's mouth to help in our battle against pollution. It's not a bad idea—what he said there. Superweasel should punish polluters in exactly the same way they are punishing the environment. That's what we did Saturday night. We smelled up Mr. Biggs, his factory and his swimming pool, but good. And we didn't do any real damage."

"Read some more, Alvin!" begged the Pest. "Please."

Just last week, Biggs had stated unequivocally to the *Daily Bugle* that his plant was *not* polluting the environment *in any manner,* and categorically denied that he was dumping any effluent into the Weasel River.

Superweasel's exploit in damming the sewer pipe caused Biggs to reconsider his former statement. When he was asked about the discharge of the plant's effluent into the river, he reluctantly announced that this had been done without his knowledge, and that he would fire those persons responsible.

"We will clear up this matter immediately," Biggs promised, "regardless of cost."

"Oh, Alvin, we did it," said the Pest. "Now the river can really be cleaned up."

"And maybe we'll be able to fish in Three Oaks Pond again before long," said Shoie.

But Alvin was interested in the last few lines of the newspaper article:

The *Daily Bugle,* on Saturday night, transmitted an article regarding Superweasel and his exploits on the Amalgamated Press wire. As a result, countless questions regarding Superweasel and his identity have been asked by other newspapers.

Under these circumstances it appears questionable whether Superweasel will make any further appearances.

Alvin folded the paper. He swung his legs over the side of the bed and sat up straight. For a moment no one said a word. Alvin broke the silence. "Well? Where will Superweasel strike next?"

"Strike next?" echoed the Pest.

"We don't dare, old bean," said Shoie. "Everybody will be looking for Superweasel now."

"Of course we dare," proclaimed Alvin. "Superweasel is the world's bravest pollution fighter!"

Alvin fed the problem into the Magnificent Brain. "Let's see, now," he said, thinking aloud. "We've struck a blow to clean up water pollution. There are, of course, other ways of polluting the environment. For example, air pollution. Superweasel must now strike a blow against air polluters."

"But who are they?" asked the Pest. "Our teacher told us it was the car drivers."

"That's true," said the Magnificent Brain dreamily. "Each car owner contributes to the air pollution."

The Pest got to her feet, thought, whirled about, and said:

"Let's go, let's go, to outer space,
To Jupiter and Mars;
We must escape this polluted place
It's ruined by our cars."

"However," Alvin went on, as though he hadn't

even heard her, "it would be difficult for Superweasel to strike back at particular car owners. Therefore he must strike at another big type of air polluter."

"Who do you mean?"

"Just think for a minute," continued the Magnificent Brain smoothly. "There is one big air polluter in this town."

Silence. Then, "I know!" exclaimed Shoie. "Mom complains every time she hangs out her wash."

"Right. Every morning the foundry, out on the west side of town, fires up its furnaces. By eight o'clock the smoke is really rolling out of that high smokestack. And the prevailing winds blow it right over Riverton."

"What does 'prevailing' mean?" asked the Pest.

"It means 'most of the time.' The wind blows from the west most of the time around here, so Riverton gets all the soot from that foundry smokestack."

"Hey, Brain! What can Superweasel possibly do to cut that kind of air pollution?"

"I don't know yet. Let's ride out to the foundry and take a look. Maybe we'll get an idea on the spot."

Mrs. Fernald was in the kitchen baking cookies, and the smell went all through the house. The kids paused just long enough for samples. When she held out a full cookie sheet, the Pest took two cookies, Alvin took five, and Shoie carefully picked up eight. Alvin's mother looked down at the cookie sheet. There was one cookie left on it. She shook her head in disbelief. Then she looked up at Alvin and said, "Where are you kids going?"

"Oh, just out for a bike ride," said Alvin.

"What about your homework? You know your father and I weren't very pleased with your last report card. Why don't you do your homework right now?"

"That's what I'm doing, Mom," replied Alvin. Before she had a chance to reply he slipped through the back door and ran for his bike.

After all, what he'd told her was the truth. He *was* going out to do his homework.

9. On Top of Old Smokey

Again it was dark, and Superweasel was out there, somewhere, roaming the night in search of the scalawags and scoundrels who pollute the planet.

Actually, Superweasel—all three of him—was just then approaching the foundry.

If anyone with especially good vision had been watching, he would have seen three small figures scurry across the parking lot and head for the big smokestack in the back of the building. The lead figure was the smallest—slim and lithe, topped by a halo of burnished gold. Behind the second figure trailed a cape, as black as the night itself. And the tallest figure was straining under the burden of a heavy pack.

The three figures reached the base of the smokestack and crouched there, panting.

Finally, "Are you ready, old bean?" It was Shoie's voice.

"Don't rush me." The words were muffled by the mask. "Are you sure you brought everything?"

"Check. The rope and the pulley are in my pack.

The other stuff is hidden over there on the edge of the parking lot. I'll go back and get it while you're climbing."

"Are you sure you aren't scared, Alvin?" asked the Pest.

"Of course I'm scared. Scared to death. But Superweasel has declared war on all polluters. If I could climb that dumb old fence out at the chemical plant, I can climb this smokestack. It even has a ladder going up it. Shoie, give me the pulley and one end of the rope."

From the depths of the pack Shoie brought forth a pulley. It was a big one, with a heavy hook on the top. Alvin reached up under his Superweasel shirt and hooked the pulley to one of his belt loops. Then he took the end of the rope and tied it to his belt. He took a deep breath.

"Ready?" asked Shoie.

Alvin didn't answer because he knew his voice would shake. Instead he reached out one hand and felt across the bricks of the smokestack until he touched one of the iron rungs that were embedded in the bricks; they had been installed to allow inspection and repair of the stack.

Alvin felt upward along the rungs until he could grip one about shoulder height. As he stepped up on the bottom rung a cold wind seemed to blow down the back of his neck.

The adventure had been planned three days ago, when they had cycled over to inspect the chimney. They had ridden around the parking lot as though they were playing bike tag. They watched the heavy black smoke belching from the smokestack.

"Wow!" said Shoie in awe. "How can we do anything about that?"

"Superweasel has superstrength," said Alvin. "See that ladder on the side? We'll use that to climb up and plug the top of the chimney."

"*Who* will climb up and plug the top of the chimney?"

There was a pause. Then Alvin said, "You will. You're the best athlete in Roosevelt School. Besides, I don't want to cheat you—it's your turn to wear the Superweasel costume."

"Oh, no! Not me! I know I'm a good athlete, but *I can't stand heights*. Just the thought of going up there scares me."

"I'll do it," offered the Pest.

Alvin thought for a moment. There was some danger involved. He couldn't let her do it. His best bet was to shame Shoie into doing it. "No. If Shoie's going to be chicken, then I'll do it myself."

"Well, I *am* chicken. I don't mind saying so. I'll do anything else, but I won't climb that smokestack."

Now, pausing with his foot on the bottom rung, Alvin realized that he didn't particularly like high places himself.

Finally Shoie said in a quiet voice, "You know, we don't *have* to do it, old man. We can go home. Nobody will ever know the difference."

"*We'll* know the difference. And in particular, *I'll*

72

know the difference. I said I'd climb it, and I will. Pest, you keep the rope from tangling while I climb. Shoie, you go back over there and get the other stuff we need. Superweasel is on his way!"

The first few rungs weren't bad—no worse than climbing the tree outside his bedroom window. After about thirty steps, he looked down.

That was a mistake. In the dim light he could see the Pest's little face looking up at him, and already she seemed a long way below.

"How are you doing, old bean?" Shoie's voice was a hoarse whisper floating up to him.

Alvin made himself answer. "Fine. Just fine. Resting here for a minute."

"Boy, I'm sure glad I'm not up there!" muttered Shoie.

Alvin wished he hadn't heard Shoie's last words. He looked up at the curved, brick stack that reached high above him.

Superweasel gritted his teeth, and took another step upward, then another, then another. Soon he found himself climbing steadily.

Even though it was a chilly spring night, the mask was getting hot. He stopped for a rest. He hung on with one hand while he shoved the mask up on top of his head. There. That helped. Now he could breathe better, and see better, too.

Suddenly he was sorry he'd pushed up the mask. He had made the mistake of glancing downward again, and the sight paralyzed him. The rope, tied to his belt, trailed down into the nothingness below. The floodlights on the parking lot looked like tiny stars. He couldn't even see his sister, or Shoie.

Alvin began feeling sick to his stomach. The streetlights of Riverton, far below, seemed to be wheeling around in big circles. He closed his eyes and hung onto the ladder with both hands, clung so hard that he began losing all feeling in his fingers. At that point he called on the Magnificent Brain for help.

"Mustn't get sick," said the M.B. Alvin took at least a dozen deep breaths of the cool night air. That helped.

"Open your eyes. Look up, but not down."

His eyes were squeezed shut so tightly that his forehead ached. He opened them a slit, and glanced upward.

Instantly he felt better. The top of the smokestack was very close above his head, no more than ten or twelve steps upward. He shook his head back and forth to clear the last of the cobwebs, then began climbing once more. At last, he felt the rough brickwork of the top of the chimney. He took one more step and looked across the top of the chimney.

Superweasel had won. He had not only conquered the smokestack, but had won his battle with himself.

Alvin was slightly surprised—and disturbed—at the smell that drifted up the stack and eddied around his head. Apparently they never let the fire in the foundry go out completely. He didn't know what kind of fuel they used, but he certainly didn't like the smell. Again he got a bit sick to his stomach.

Superweasel knew he couldn't stay there long, in those fumes atop the smokestack, so he went to work. He was hampered by his costume, and by the fact that he had to hang on with one hand while working with the other. He fumbled with the pulley, getting it off his belt loop, and hooked it to the top rung of the ladder.

He had difficulty untying the rope from his belt with just one hand. To solve the problem, he first pulled up some slack so he could poke the rope under the thumb of the hand that held onto the ladder. Then, ignoring the knot in the rope, he simply unbuckled his belt and jerked it loose from his pants. The knot slid off the belt. However, the belt whipped through the night air like a snake, gave a loud snap, and went sailing off into the blackness.

Instantly Superweasel's pants—and his own, too—began falling. He grabbed them with one hand, holding onto the ladder and the rope in a death grip with the other. He clung there momentarily, trying to figure out what to do.

The Magnificent Brain came through with its analysis, clearly, inevitably, step by step:

"1. You can't do your work and hold onto your pants at the same time. 2. It will be impossible for you to climb down the ladder while holding up your pants. 3. Therefore, both pairs of pants must go."

Having made this coldly analytical decision, the Magnificent Brain turned over the execution of the plan to Alvin. There was a reluctant pause. Then

Alvin let go of his pants and wiggled his hips. His pants fell to his ankles. He reached down and freed one leg, then the other.

The pants went sailing downward through the blackness. Alvin listened for what seemed a full minute.

"Ooooooooofffff!" The exclamation wasn't even a whisper, but a full-throated roar.

Superweasel started laughing, almost hysterically. He knew what had happened. Shoie had been standing there, peering straight up at the top of the chimney. Suddenly a big black *thing* came swooping out of the night sky like some huge prehistoric bat, and caught him full in the face.

Alvin's case of the giggles made him feel better. He threaded the end of the rope through the pulley, then began feeding the end of the rope back down to the ground below. As the rope ran over the pulley, each turn of the wheel produced a screeching sound that seemed to go out across town as though it was broadcast from a loudspeaker.

We're sure to be caught, thought Alvin. *We should have oiled the pulley. Well, I might as well go ahead with our plan.* He pulled vigorously on the rope with his one free hand, feeding the end of it toward the ground.

Finally the rope came to a stop. He knew what had happened. The loose end of the rope—the one that had been tied to his belt—had come snaking down out of the night sky. Now the rope ran from the ground, up over the pulley, and back down to the ground again. The Pest had grabbed both ends and held them, as a signal to Alvin that they were ready for the next step. Shoie now could tie materials to one end of the rope, haul on the other end, and the materials would rise up to Superweasel.

The pulley began screeching under its load. Soon, rising majestically out of the blackness, the big black cylinder they had made out of a roll of roofing paper brushed Alvin's jacket and came to rest against the pulley.

Alvin, hanging on desperately with one hand, used the other to push the roll up and over the rim of the smokestack until it lay there on top. Then he pulled at the slipknot Shoie had tied in the rope, loosened the noose, and slipped it off the tar paper roll. He fed the rope back down toward the ground. Immediately the pulley began squeaking again.

When the rope once more reached the ground, Alvin went to work on the roll of tar paper. He had trouble holding it on the rim of the chimney. Finally he grabbed the edge of it in his teeth. Then, taking a deep snort of air, he gave the roll a push. It disappeared across the top of the chimney as the paper unrolled. An instant later there was a tremendous tug on his jaws, and Alvin thought every one of his teeth would be pulled loose. He grabbed the end of the paper with his free hand.

The heavy paper now was completely unrolled, and had sealed off the top of the chimney. It balanced there.

At that moment he again felt something brush

against his sleeve. The second load of supplies had climbed up to Superweasel. It consisted of two old pieces of lumber about four feet long and a cloth banner which had been carefully prepared and rolled up in the clubhouse the day before.

Alvin waggled the boards across the rim until they lay atop the center of the chimney. He untied the rope. Then he slid one board to each side. Now the boards anchored the roofing paper to the chimney top. It would indeed take a strong wind to blow the paper away.

The chimney was sealed. Perhaps it wasn't airtight, but most of the smoke would back up into the foundry below. Superweasel's work was done—except for one thing. He placed the end of the banner under one of the two boards, then let it unfurl down the side of the smokestack.

Alvin gave the prearranged signal—two tugs on the rope. He waited for about thirty seconds, then pulled the rope back through the pulley and dropped it. He hoped Shoie and the Pest remembered to stand clear of the chimney. He was in too big a hurry to do anything about the pulley, which was an old one anyway. He simply left it where it was, hooked to the top of the ladder.

Superweasel began his dangerous descent. He paused just once, about halfway down, but had enough sense to keep his eyes on the stars.

Before long he was standing breathless between Shoie and the Pest.

"Great work, old bean," whispered Shoie, pounding him on the back.

"Why did you take off your pants, Alvin?" asked the Pest.

Alvin suddenly felt very tired. He wanted, more than anything else, to get home and into his own bed. "Tell you later," he said.

Shoie had just finished coiling the rope, and was stuffing it back into his knapsack, on top of Alvin's two pairs of pants, when they heard the scuffle of footsteps on the concrete.

"Run!" said Alvin.

Shoie and the Pest ran one way, and Alvin ran the other. As he ran, he jerked the mask down over his face. He heard the footsteps pounding along behind him, gaining ground.

"Wait!" called a voice urgently. "I won't hurt you."

Alvin slowed, and so did the footsteps. There had been something familiar about the voice.

"It's me, Superweasel. Al Moser of the *Daily Bugle*. I just want to talk to you."

Alvin stopped running and waited there, puffing, in the moonlight.

"How did you know I was here?" Alvin asked suspiciously.

"Just had a hunch you might be. The foundry is the second biggest polluter in town, so I figured you'd appear here next. I've been out here until midnight every night for three nights, waiting for you."

"You mean you were watching all the time I was climbing the chimney, and—and—"

"Yep. But I couldn't see what you were doing up on top. I can guess though. By golly, Superweasel, I've got to hand it to you. You'd never find me climbing all the way to the top of that chimney in a million years. Did you succeed?"

"Come around tomorrow morning when the first shift goes to work, and you'll see plenty of excitement."

"Superweasel, tell me the truth. Did you do any damage inside the foundry?"

Alvin shook his head. "No damage. I promised you that. Remember?"

There was a long pause. Then Moser said in a low voice, "Am I right? Did you plug the top of the smokestack?"

"Yes." Alvin said it in his own voice, proudly.

Moser shook his head admiringly. He lifted an arm as though in salute, but it was the arm that held his camera.

"What happened to your pants, Superweasel?" Moser asked softly.

Superweasel was looking down at his skinny legs just as the flashbulb went off.

10. Superhero of the Town

"SUPERWEASEL STRIKES AGAIN!" shouted the banner headline in the *Daily Bugle*.

"Wow!" exclaimed Alvin. "Look at that!"

The three kids were inside the clubhouse. Alvin was sitting on an orange crate, and Shoie and the Pest were seated side by side on the dirt floor. Alvin had paid his own money for the paper (he wanted the clippings for his scrapbook so everybody could look them over when he became president). He spread the paper across an old packing box that served as a table.

"Look at those pictures!" he said.

The other two climbed to their feet and leaned over his shoulder.

The largest photo on the front page showed workers scrambling to escape through the front door of the foundry. Behind them rolled a tremendous cloud of dirty black smoke.

Another photo, smaller and toward the bottom of the page, showed a man climbing up the smokestack. He was almost at the top, and he obviously had been assigned the job of removing the tar paper cover. Just above his head was the banner that Alvin had draped down from the chimney top. In huge letters it said exactly the same thing as the headline: "Superweasel Strikes Again!"

As Alvin turned the page, the Pest let out a squeal of laughter. Shoie fell to the floor and rolled around helplessly in the dust.

There, toward the bottom of the second page, was another photo, this one of Superweasel. His mask was in place, his cape was flowing grandly down his back, and the letters across his chest stood out in bold relief. But he wasn't wearing any pants.

"Okay, you guys," thundered Alvin, his face crimson. "Okay. That's enough. I didn't see either of you climbing that chimney last night."

With great effort Shoie and the Pest controlled their laughter. When the clubhouse was quiet again (except for an occasional eruption of the giggles from the Pest) Alvin began reading the article bylined by Mr. Moser:

Superweasel—that mysterious caped crusader—struck again last night in his continuing battle against the polluters of Riverton.

The pollution fighter managed to climb unseen to the top of the smokestack at the Blaha Foundry, haul up the necessary supplies, and plug the smokestack so the smoke backed up inside the building below.

The foundry has long been the subject of complaints by Riverton citizens.

This reporter interviewed Merle J. Blaha, the owner, at the foundry this morning. Blaha expressed bitterness against the "criminal" who had plugged his smokestack. When asked about installation of antipollution equipment Blaha said, "It's a matter of principle. No criminal can tell me how to run my foundry."

Despite his emphatic statement, a truck delivered antipollution equipment to the foundry this morning. Workmen immediately began installing it.

It is apparent that Superweasel again has succeeded in his battle against pollution, this time where city officials have failed more than once.

"Hey," shouted Shoie, "we won the fight!"

"Of course we did," said Alvin calmly. "Superweasel *always* wins."

"Look!" said the Pest. "It says: 'See the Superweasel editorial on page 5.' "

Alvin eagerly flipped the pages of the paper. The editorial was short and to the point.

The *Daily Bugle* can find no fault in what Superweasel has been doing in this community. No one has been hurt, and no property has been damaged.

On the other hand, whenever Superweasel has set his sights on a polluter, his actions have been effective. The water pollution level in the Weasel River has been drastically reduced, and there is hope that fish and other forms of wildlife soon will reappear in the stream and along its banks.

Last night's daring action by Superweasel has dramatically reduced the air pollution over Riverton.

Superweasel is as effective as those other legendary

crime fighters: Superman, Batman and Spiderman.

As long as Riverton's crimefighter does not resort to vandalism, his work will have, not just the approval, but the enthusiastic endorsement of the *Daily Bugle*.

Superweasel is making Riverton a better town for every resident. A citizen might well ask, as they did of the Lone Ranger, "Who was that masked man? I wanted to thank him."

Who is Superweasel? No one knows who he is—but our thoughts and our hopes go with him.

Shoie gave a long low whistle. "Makes you feel like some kind of a hero, doesn't it?"

"Except that we're not getting any of the credit," replied Alvin.

"There's no need for any more secrecy," suggested Shoie. "Tomorrow let's tell Miss Miles and all the kids in class that we are Superweasel, and that we've been doing this as our antipollution project. Why, we'll be heroes of the whole school, even superheroes of the whole town."

Alvin considered the idea. He had to admit that it appealed to him. One of his weaknesses was that he liked to be the center of attention. And he certainly would get a lot of attention if he announced that he was the mighty pollution fighter.

But something deep inside made him reluctant to expose Superweasel's identity just yet.

"I think," he said slowly, "that Superweasel should strike out against one other kind of pollution before he hangs up his mask and cape for good."

There was a moment of silence. Then the Pest asked, "What other kind of pollution is there, Alvin?"

"Yeah," said Shoie, puzzled. "Superweasel has fought air pollution and water pollution. What else can he do?"

"Plenty," said Alvin quietly. "But let's not rush into anything. Let's plan something *really* big, something that will change the whole town, something that will make people remember Superweasel for years to come. I have an idea or two, but I want to feed them through the old M.B. and see what comes out."

"Tell us," begged the Pest.

"No. Not yet. But let's meet again tomorrow afternoon. Maybe we can start planning Superweasel's greatest adventure of all."

11. Superweasel Is a Bum

But the next day something went wrong.

Very, very wrong.

Instead of superheroes, the kids found themselves superbums. The *Daily Bugle* carried a different headline:

SUPERWEASEL VANDALIZES DOWNTOWN STORES

The article, bylined by Mr. Moser, stated that two store windows had been broken with bricks the night before, and that Superweasel had scrawled his name in spray paint across each of the stores. Furthermore, a masked and costumed figure had been seen fleeing down an alley near the scene of the crimes.

The seriousness of the situation startled Alvin. The Magnificent Brain boggled at the thought of what had happened. "Boy, are we in trouble!" he exclaimed when the three kids met in the tree house.

"Who could have done it?" asked Shoie.

"I dunno." There was a long pause. Then Alvin asked, in a voice as natural as he could make it, "What were you doing last night, Shoie?"

"I studied. Watched TV. Went to bed early. I was tired. Why?"

"Just wondered."

"How about you?" Was there a touch of suspicion in Shoie's voice? "Where were you last night?"

"Same as you."

The two boys stared at each other.

"The Superweasel costume is in the clubhouse," stated Alvin. "In your backyard."

"That costume is too small for me. You're the only one it fits."

"How do I know?"

"Hey, you guys!" The Pest's high little voice cut into them accusingly. "What's the matter with you— both of you? When the least little thing goes wrong, you guys start blaming each other." She paused, then said indignantly, "We all know that nobody here would do it—would even *want* to do it. So it *has* to be somebody else. Snap out of it, you guys."

Alvin and Shoie looked at each other. They both started grinning sheepishly. Alvin held out his fist, thumb sticking up, and Shoie grabbed it. Simultaneously all three kids intoned, "Power to Superweasel!"

"Okay," said Alvin. "So we know nobody here did it. But that doesn't solve our basic problem. Let's analyze the situation scientifically. First, we know that somebody else impersonated Superweasel. Second, that person performed criminal acts—broke windows and

88

sprayed paint on private property." He paused, thinking.

"What comes third, Alvin?" asked his sister.

"Well, third is mighty serious. Has it occurred to either of you that now we'll be in very deep trouble if we let people know we are Superweasel?"

"You're right," said Shoie.

"We might even end up in jail." The Pest spoke in a small, frightened voice.

Mr. Moser isn't going to like Superweasel after this." Shoie was thinking out loud.

"No. And if we get any more publicity, it will be exactly the wrong kind."

"The police will be trying to capture Superweasel," whispered the Pest. "Even Daddy will be trying to find us. Oh, Alvin what can we do?"

Silence again. Finally Alvin declared forcefully, "There's only one thing we *can* do. We can forget about the guy who's doing the damage. We won't waste even one second of our time on that criminal. Instead, we'll plan the biggest antipollution drive *that's ever been seen anywhere on the face of the earth*. And Superweasel will supervise the whole thing. When everyone sees how much good he is doing, they'll *know* he couldn't have broken those windows."

"What's this plan of yours, old bean?" Shoie said, his spirits rising.

"First of all, we know a lot of kids around town. Agreed?"

"Sure. What's that got to do with it?"

"Do you think, among the three of us, that we know at least one kid in all four other grade schools? A kid we *really can trust?*"

Shoie and the Pest thought for a moment. "I think so," said Shoie. "Why?"

"We're going to organize every fourth, fifth and sixth grader in town. That's hundreds and hundreds of kids. And maybe, on the big day, *other* kids will join *those* kids. We're going to organize the kids without a single adult knowing anything about it. Just the kids, all over town, doing their thing for their environment. And supervising the whole operation will be—*Superweasel!* Why, the whole state, maybe even the whole country, will take notice. Why, why—" when the Magnificent Brain started rolling, it frequently went completely out of control, "—why, I wouldn't even be surprised if the president himself hears about Superweasel. Maybe we'll even get medals and things!"

The Pest's eyes were shining. "Oh, Alvin! Tell us what you want us to do!"

"We've got to get organized," said Alvin loftily, "that's the secret of the whole thing. First we'll draw up a list of names, so we can contact one kid in each of the schools. Then we'll write a letter to each of those kids. Let's see, now. We'd better make our big day a week from this Saturday. Meanwhile as far as the adults in town will know, Superweasel will be out of action."

90

12. Double Trouble

But to Alvin's horror, Superweasel *wasn't* out of action. He continued his spree of vandalism.

Damage was reported in the paper almost every night; and each time, the name Superweasel was scrawled across the vandalized property. One night, two tires were slashed; another night a statue was overturned in the park; on two successive nights garbage was strewn across cars, porches and public buildings.

By now the citizens of Riverton were downright angry. "That Superweasel guy better not come around here," growled Mr. Otto, the butcher, "or I'll grind him into hamburger."

Many residents began to leave their porch lights on all night, and installed extra locks on their doors. The Police Department was swamped with calls from hysterical people who imagined they saw masked animal-figures everywhere. Alvin's dad had to work extra hours each day so police patrols could be extended.

"For the first time in my life," Alvin said to Shoie, a week after the first appearance of the impostor, "I feel totally helpless. If we announce that we are Superweasel, then everybody will blame us for all the damage that's been done. And if we don't say anything about it, then whoever is pretending to be Superweasel will go right on doing more and more damage."

The kids again were in Alvin's room. The Pest was sitting primly at the desk, trying to write letters and listen at the same time. They had decided that, because her handwriting was by far the neatest, she should write the letters seeking help from kids in other schools. Alvin had already written a rough letter for her to copy.

"Alvin, maybe we should cancel our plans for one more Superweasel adventure," suggested Shoie. "You've heard what's happening. Everybody in town is complaining, and everybody's suspicious of everybody else. Instead of doing good, Superweasel is ruining this town. Maybe we'd better cool it."

Alvin shook his head. "We can't cool it—not as long as that lousy impostor keeps scrawling Superweasel's name across his dirty work. The only thing we can do is to make the town aware, once again, that the *real* Superweasel is a good guy who only wants to fight pollution." Alvin's voice grew stronger as he talked. "Pest," he ordered, "read us that letter, so we'll know it says exactly what we want it to say."

She picked up the paper in front of her. "Okay, here goes. 'My dearest Duke:' That's the way I started out because this one goes to Duke McDonald in the fifth grade at Field School. Shoie knows him because they went to camp together, and I think he's the cutest boy I ever saw so I thought—"

"No, Pest. Just say, 'Dear Duke.' Now read the letter itself."

Dear Duke: You are one of four kids chosen for a special job because I know you can keep a secret. If you can't keep a secret, don't read any further. Just destroy this letter, because otherwise some kids might get hurt, and neither of us would want that.

First, I'll let you in on a secret. I—Superweasel—am an imaginary character invented by kids as a means of fighting pollution. I've never done anything wrong in my life as Superweasel. Somebody else is using my name so I'll get the blame for the vandalism in Riverton.

I need your help in the biggest attack on pollution that this town—or any other town—has ever seen. If you want to help, meet me in the little park behind the library Thursday night at 9:30 sharp.

Don't mention this note to anyone!

Signed: Superweasel.

The Pest gasped. "I just realized that I wrote the letter, and it's in my handwriting, and if anybody notices it I'll be blamed for all the bad things that have been going on, and maybe I'll go to prison."

"Don't worry, Sis. Everything's going to come out okay. Now copy off that same letter to Loopy Ebright and Ellie Deroo and Dick Dempe. Shoie, have you figured out yet how you can deliver the letters without being seen?"

"Sure. We'll put the kids' names on the envelopes and mark them 'SECRET AND PERSONAL.' I'll slip them into their school lockers this afternoon."

"I hope none of the kids gives us away," said Alvin. "We might be arrested on the spot Thursday night. And it might be Dad who makes the arrest!"

Alvin tried not to let the others know how worried he really was.

Every day, from then on, was worse than the preceding one.

And the bad days came to a climax on Thursday afternoon. The Pest was waiting on the front steps when their paper boy sailed the *Daily Bugle* in her general direction. She leaped high in the air and snatched it with a one-hand catch. Alvin and Shoie were watching from the bedroom window, and gave her a rousing cheer.

But there was nothing to cheer about when she appeared breathless at the door, moments later.

"*Look!*" was all she could say. She pointed to a big picture across the front page.

It was a picture of Superweasel! His face was hidden by a mask, a velvet cape flowed down his back, and his chest bore the now-familiar letters. In his hand he held a spray can, and he was spraying "Superweasel" in bold letters across the brick wall that ran around the county museum.

"CAUGHT IN THE ACT" said the headline. Mr. Moser's article stated that he was on his way home from work late the night before, and had happened to walk past the museum. He had noticed the strange figure of Superweasel in the process of disfiguring the wall. He had promptly taken a flash picture with the camera he always carried. As soon as the bulb went off, Superweasel dropped the can of paint and ran, escaping down an alley.

"Where did he get the costume?" whispered the Pest.

Alvin thought long and hard. "Well, Pest didn't make it for him, that's for sure. And I'm no split personality, like Dr. Jekyl and Mr. Hyde."

"Alvin, you *don't* have any split personality," said Shoie, "though sometimes I think you're a bit cracked."

"There's only one answer," said Alvin, beginning to perk up, now that he knew the other two kids had faith in him. "Pest, how did you make the costume? Was there a pattern, or anything like that?"

"No. I just sort of eyeballed it."

"If you eyeballed it, then someone else can eyeball it too. Superweasel's picture has appeared in the paper twice for anyone to see. Once on the fence by the chemical plant, and once by the foundry without—well, without any pants."

"That's right!" exclaimed Shoie. "He made it himself."

"Well, what are we going to do about it?" wailed the Pest. "I feel like burning that dumb costume."

"No. Don't do that. The fact that someone else is running around in a Superweasel costume just makes it all the more obvious that we have to clear Superweasel's name. Now, more than ever, we have to go ahead with our plans." Alvin's voice turned crisp. "I'm going to meet those four kids behind the library to-night."

"I'm not so sure you should do that," said Shoie doubtfully. He pointed to the *Daily Bugle*. "And I'm not so sure any of the kids will be there—after they see the paper."

"Superweasel will be there," declared Alvin, "in full costume!"

13. The Superplan Unfolds

Bzzzzzzzzzzzz. SLAP!

Early spring mosquitoes were holding a convention on Alvin's nose. Angrily he slapped them away, then quickly pulled down his Superweasel mask. "Doggone bugs!"

"Stand still!" the Pest whispered. She was trying to tie the velvet cape around his neck.

The three kids were hiding in the tall bushes that grew along one side of the library.

And Alvin was scared. Just about as scared as he'd been on the way up the smokestack. He knew that the costume would be convincing evidence against him. The police would brand him a criminal, guilty of all the vandalism in Riverton for the past two weeks. No one would ever believe the truth—that another Superweasel, costumed exactly like Alvin, was stalking the streets of the town. Somehow Alvin had to find the false caped crusader and expose him.

He slapped cautiously at a mosquito on the back of his neck. He missed it, and a moment later he could

hear it buzzing like a chainsaw around the nose-hole in his mask.

Suddenly he forgot the mosquito. Shoie had grabbed his shoulder, and was pointing out through the bushes at a picnic table in the little park behind the library. There was one small bulb burning off to the side, and in the dim light, Alvin could see two figures approaching the table. His heart began to pound, but he waited. Finally another figure came up the path, then still another.

At least all four kids had come. But was it a trap? Had they told their parents, or the police, about the meeting? Were the police surrounding the park *right now?*

He shouldered his way out of the bushes, waving wildly at the swarm of mosquitoes. In one hand he held four white envelopes.

Alvin Fernald paused for a moment. He pulled back his shoulders and lifted his head. Then he strode across the grass toward the four kids seated at the picnic table. One of them—a boy about his own age—glanced up, and immediately sprang to his feet. The other kids looked around. As Alvin approached the girl sitting at the table shrank back.

"Don't be scared," said Alvin. But he himself was scared. If this was a trap, the police would pounce right now. "I'm glad you accepted my invitation."

"Who are you, anyway?" asked one of the boys suspiciously. "Why, you aren't even as big as I am. For such a short kid you sure have been doing a lot of damage around town."

"Not true," said Alvin. "There is another Super-weasel—an impostor who dresses just like me—who has been doing the damage. All I've been doing is fighting pollution."

"Can you prove that?" asked the girl.

Alvin sighed. For the first time he spoke in his own, his normal, voice. "Maybe there's no way I can convince you, but I swear I haven't done any vandalism. Listen, kids. I'm just about your own age. Two of you know me slightly, the other two know friends of mine. Soon you'll find out who I am. Right now I'm in trouble. I need your help in finding and exposing the impostor. Even more important, I need your help in the biggest antipollution campaign any town has ever seen. *We can do a lot of good if you'll work with me.* What do you say?"

The biggest boy grunted. "Sounds mighty screwy to me. You say you need help. Well, you won't get any help from me until I find out who you are." He took a step toward Alvin. "And maybe the easiest way to do that is to rip the mask right off your face."

Alvin held up one hand. In a voice so commanding it startled even him, he ordered, "Stop! If you rip off my mask you'll ruin a lot of fun for hundreds of other kids, and a lot of good for Riverton. If you'll just trust me—and help me—I guarantee you'll be the talk of the town. You'll be its heroes, too. Now, what do you say?"

The girl spoke up. "How long do we have to trust you?"

"Only until Saturday night. Then you'll find out

everything there is to know about Superweasel." He lowered his voice, pleading now. "Please, won't you help?"

The four kids looked at each other. It was the girl who finally said, "I guess it won't hurt us to listen to your plan. We have to do *something* about pollution. If your plan sounds like a good one, I'll help. But I'm not going to do anything that's against the law."

"Of course not!" Superweasel's voice sounded truly horrified. It was that, more than anything else, which persuaded the three boys. They nodded their heads.

"What do you want us to do?" asked the girl, now taking command of the group. "What kind of pollution are we fighting?"

"What kind of pollution is the most widespread of all?" asked Superweasel in return.

"Air."

"Water."

"No. Neither one. The most widespread form of pollution is *littering*."

None of the kids seemed very excited over that. "You mean all you want us to do is put our waste-paper in a trash can?" asked one of the boys in disgust.

"No. Much more than that. I want you to get every kid—*every single kid*—in the fourth, fifth and sixth grades of your schools, organized *in total secrecy*. We can't let adults know anything about it, or the whole effect will be ruined. You've got to organize the kids into teams, with team leaders. This tells you how to do it." Alvin plopped the four envelopes on the table. "We'll strike at exactly 7:30 Saturday night. I might mention that Alvin Fernald and Shoie Shoemaker, from Roosevelt School, are already in on the plan." Seeing the lack of enthusiasm on their faces, Alvin went rapidly on, "Now here's what I'm asking you to do. First I want you to—"

Fifteen minutes later there was no longer any sign of doubt on the faces of the kids. Instead there was excitement. The kids were asking questions, making suggestions, arguing about how best to do the job. They had discovered that they were to be the key figures in what probably would be the biggest day in the history of Riverton.

14. What's Going on Here?

Superweasel had set 7:30 Saturday night as the moment of his final and most spectacular achievement. Long before 7:30, a good many citizens of Riverton noticed some highly unusual activity around town.

1:15 P.M.   A widow on the east side of town calls the police and reports in a hysterical voice, "The hippies are rioting across the street!" Sergeant Fernald and Officer Twilley are dispatched to investigate. Approximately a hundred children of grade school age are milling around one girl, who is giving orders. The kids break up into orderly groups. As the puzzled officers are about to report back to headquarters, their squad-car radio squawks into life. . . .

1:26 P.M.   The officers are ordered to investigate a disturbance at 1056 South Oak Street. "A white male, approximately twelve years old, is passing out subversive literature on his front lawn."

At the scene of the alleged crime the officers find another large group of children in line approaching an owl-eyed boy, who is seated behind a wooden box. He hands each child an envelope. The officers seize one of the envelopes as evidence, and look inside. A piece of paper bears the scrawled message, "One-half block, including the alley, just south of the Kwik-Bite Burger Stand." It is hardly a subversive message. The officers climb back into their squad car.

2:42 P.M. A woman in a house on the north edge of town gleefully telephones her husband at his job.

"Calm down!" he shouts at her. "Just tell me what happened."

"Remember how, for two weeks, I've been trying to get Tim to clean up all that junk in the yard? The dead leaves, tin cans, and old newspapers? Well, a few minutes ago I looked out the window. You won't believe this, but *Tim not only cleaned up our yard, but then he went across the street with two other kids and cleaned up the vacant lot.* I tell you, we've misjudged that child. Bring home some peppermint ice cream. That's his favorite."

3:10 P.M. A twelve-year-old from Roosevelt School is sent to his room by his mother. This time he really has goofed. He thought the bedspread hanging on the line was just an old rag. He could find no boxes to pack litter in, so he took down the "old rag" and spread it out in the muddy backyard. Then he began throwing trash onto it that had been accumulating since the founder of Riverton galloped into the area 150 years ago and tossed a rusty old horseshoe into the bushes. As a matter of fact, the boy picked up one remaining nail of that horseshoe, wondered briefly what it was, and then tossed it onto his mother's best bedspread with all the other trash. Just then his mother appeared at the door and began hollering. . . .

3:55 P.M.   A small boy gazes upward into a huge elm tree. There, in the topmost branches, are the remnants of last-year's kite. He has been instructed to bring in *every bit of scrap* in his half-block. He starts climbing. . . .

4:03 P.M.   The Fire Department is called to rescue a small boy caught in the topmost branches of a tall elm tree.

5:43 P.M.   Al Perry calls City Hall with a special problem. It is Saturday afternoon, so he has gone, as is his custom on this day of the week, to Orgo's Orgy for a "bit of liquid refreshment." Three hours later, ready at last to go home, he heads across the Orgy's parking lot and finds his dump truck piled high with everything from bent bedsprings to a weatherworn outhouse which, for fifteen years, has been the biggest eyesore on the south side of town.

"What," Al Perry asks City Hall, "should I do with the trash in my truck?" When the City Hall operator, trying to handle a flood of incoming calls, accidentally breaks the connection, he gently replaces the phone on the hook and heads back across the parking lot toward Orgo's Orgy.

6:06 P.M.   Because of the obvious unrest throughout town, the police chief cancels all police leaves, and orders the entire force to report for duty. "Something's wrong," he tells Sergeant Fernald. "I can feel it in my bones."

6:15 P.M.   In his office Mayor Homer Bienfang is trying to decide what to do. He is new at this job (he

was elected only two months ago) and he has no idea how to deal with civil unrest.

Mayor Bienfang gulps down two more aspirin. All kinds of things have gone wrong, just since he took office. First it was a wave of vandalism caused by that awful Superweasel. Now the kids are up to some kind of deviltry.

Mayor Bienfang has never had any children of his own, and he has no idea how to handle kids. Instead of causing all this trouble, why can't they do something constructive, like decorating store windows on Halloween?

He begins studying a row of figures on a sheet of paper in front of him. It shows that Riverton has 3,281 children under fifteen years of age. The thought of 3,281 children totally out of control within his city terrifies the mayor.

He reaches into a drawer and pulls a sheet of paper from a file marked SECRET. The heading across the top of the paper reads: "From the Office of the Governor. To all Mayors of this State. Subject: How to Call Out the National Guard in Time of Civil Unrest."

Mayor Bienfang studies the paper, then makes a courageous decision. He replaces the sheet in the SECRET file. He leans down and puts his head on his desk.

15. The Junk Parade

Dusk was falling on an uneasy Riverton. Children were called in for supper. Streetlights blinked into life.

The first ripple of the evening's activities came from the outer edges of town. Superweasel had set 7:30 as *the moment;* kids on the far edges of town had to start first in order to reach the city square at that time.

As if on signal, block by block, kids gathered for a moment under the streetlights, then scattered to their backyards and alleys. When they reappeared, each was lurching along under a heavy load of trash. Some carried it in plastic bags, others hauled it in wagons, still others simply dragged it along.

One girl borrowed her little brother's baby buggy, loaded it with rusty tin cans and old chunks of concrete, and pushed it out into the street to lead the procession toward City Hall.

Behind her came a boy with a huge picnic basket under each arm, one loaded with garbage, the other with broken bottles.

One of the strongest boys in Madison School was balancing a huge cardboard box on top of his head. The box held a broken barber pole, a dozen paint cans, two splintered folding chairs, and a batch of newspapers still soggy from the previous night's rain. It was the wet newspapers that weakened the box. At the corner of Oak and 1st Street, the bottom suddenly gave way, and the boy found his head thrust up inside. Thick red paint oozed down his forehead.

The nine kids who had, for years, called themselves the Dirty Ears Gang had "borrowed" a trailer from one of their garages and loaded it with junk from every vacant lot east of Main Street. Now four boys pulled on each side of the trailer tongue like horses in harness, while the ninth member of the Dirty Ears Gang pushed from behind. Going down the Maple Street hill the gang lost control of the trailer, and it started rolling along under its own power, gradually gathering speed. Suddenly it hit a bump, veered to the right, blundered up a driveway, across a widow's lawn, and knocked down half a dozen old fence posts as though they were bowling pins. The widow, who had been trying to hire someone to remove the posts for more than a month, stood on her porch and cheered. The Dirty Ears finally recovered the trailer, tossed the fence posts into it with the rest of the trash, and eased their way to the bottom of the hill.

Two of the larger boys picked up a rusty old swing-set and carted it down the alley toward Willow Avenue. In the semidarkness they failed to see a low-hanging telephone wire, and the swing-set snapped it cleanly in two. At that very moment a woman's hysterical voice was telling the Police Department by phone that she had seen a gang of hoodlums roaming the alley behind her home. She was cut off in midsentence, and locked herself in her bathroom.

Her message had been noted, however. The police duty officer dispatched Sergeant Fernald and Officer Twilley to investigate what was going on along Second Street near Willow.

Plenty was going on. Willow Avenue is fairly close to the downtown area of Riverton, so by the time the baby buggy leading the parade reached Willow, at least three hundred kids were following. And by now they weren't all grade school kids. The parade seemed to attract all ages from kindergartners to high school kids. They moved an incredible amount of junk gleaned from the entire east end of town.

Evil Eye Davis, Willy Davis's little brother, was sprawled atop his own wagon holding down a load of unwrapped garbage while Willy pulled it toward City Hall. Theresa Undermine carried her baby sister, sucking on a bottle, under one arm and a shopping basket full of everything from gum wrappers to a dead cat under the other.

Sergeant Fernald wheeled the police car around the corner and onto Willow Avenue. Instantly he slammed on his brakes. Advancing toward him through the semidarkness was a horde of kids, totally blocking the street and overflowing onto the sidewalks. In the lead was a red-haired girl pushing a baby buggy piled high with junk. Just behind her marched a preschool boy in baggy pants beating a drum made from a rusty bucket. All the other kids were trying to keep in step despite the drummer's short steps.

It was like an army of huge ants. Nothing could stop the march, and the kids engulfed the squad car. They flowed, irresistibly, right on around it. Sergeant Fernald rolled down the window and started shouting.

That was where he made his mistake. Coming directly at the squad car at that moment were half a dozen kids, each gripping the edge of a big sheet of plastic. On top of the plastic, in a huge ugly wad, was all of the overflow garbage from the Hoosier Hot Dog Haven out on East Main Street, which had a reputation for leaving garbage strewn about. As Sergeant Fernald thrust his head out the window and shouted, he almost rubbed noses with a skinny little girl. Startled by his sudden appearance and loud shout, she shied away, bumping into the boy next to her. Instantly scores of kids went down like rows of dominoes. The garbage on top of the plastic sheet slooped toward the squad car, and then hurtled like an avalanche down onto the windshield. Ketchup streamed across the glass. Sergeant Fernald surrendered; he just sat there and watched the parade flow past his window.

Three kids rolled old tires from curb to curb. One girl wore a bashed-in motorcycle helmet and carried a huge bouquet of mangled artificial flowers. Six bigger boys carried the broken football goalposts that had been rotting on the ground since the high school team had moved to a new practice field.

And (unbelievable!) here came at least thirty kids carrying on their shoulders the ancient Volkswagen that had been an eyesore in the ditch along Taylor Road for five years or more. Inside the car, sitting proudly in the driver's seat, was a seven-year-old boy peering intently through thick glasses at the shattered windshield, whipping the steering wheel this way and that, and shouting instructions.

Four boys carried an old bathtub full of the two-year-old Klemm triplets, who were having the time of their lives. Half a dozen girls marched proudly along carrying an old chicken coop that shed a gentle stream of feathers like a soft snowfall, blanketing the marchers just behind.

Five minutes later, when the last of the parade had ebbed past, Sergeant Fernald discovered that the kids who had been carrying the sheet of plastic had stayed behind to clean up the mess. Eagerly they spread the plastic sheet on the pavement, and scraped the squad car as clean as they could, piling the trash back on the sheet.

Sergeant Fernald approached the red-headed girl, who had pushed her baby buggy to one side and stayed behind to help clean up the squad car. "Young lady, tell me about this. What are you kids doing?"

"Cleaning up the environment." She said it proudly. "Picking up every bit of junk and trash we can find anywhere. We're trying to show you grown-ups what a mess you've made of our town for so many years." There was a pause. Then she admitted thoughtfully, "Sometimes kids make messes, too. Anyway, we're cleaning up the whole city. Look around tomorrow and you won't see any litter *anywhere*."

"Where are you taking all the trash?"

"Down to City Hall. We're going to sort it there, and dump it in big piles. We figure that if we gather it all together in one place, then the adults will *have* to dispose of it."

Sergeant Fernald's eyes twinkled. "I think you're right. Whose idea was this?"

"Superweasel's." It popped out before she thought, and she clapped her hand over her mouth. "Ooooooooohh! I shouldn't have said that! Please don't tell anybody."

As the kids picked up the plastic sheet and marched away, Sergeant Fernald reached for his microphone.

"Squad One calling headquarters. Request that the chief be put on the line."

"I hear you, Sergeant. What's going on?"

Alvin Fernald's father took a deep breath. "Well, I think we can be proud of the kids in this town, sir. They're a lot more aware of their environment than most of the adults." He described what was happening. "They should be coming into your sight just about now. I suggest we play it loose, sir. Let the kids do their work and have their fun. Keep members of the police force out of sight. Oh, and I suggest you call the mayor and tell him what's happening, sir. It will ease his mind."

"I'll do that. Whose idea was this whole operation?"

Sergeant Fernald was silent for a moment. Then, "The kids say it was Superweasel's idea."

Obviously the chief was thinking that over. "Well, we have a score to settle with that guy, whoever he is. He could clean up the streets of Heaven, and we'd still track him down for the vandalism he's done. Instinct tells me we'll nail him tonight. Report back here, Sergeant. Over and out."

"Over and out."

Suddenly, for no apparent reason, Sergeant Fernald was a troubled man. He had, within his own mind, admired Superweasel for his antipollution efforts. He had admired him, that is, until the vandalism began. It was almost as though Superweasel were two different persons. . . .

Sergeant Fernald climbed into the squad car and headed for City Hall.

16. At the City Hall

An owl, soaring high through the night air over Riverton, would have been able to see four long columns of kids snaking through town, marching on City Hall from the four major points of the compass.

Alvin, Shoie and the Pest were waiting on the curbstone when the West Main Street column came into view. Some of the kids from Roosevelt School shouted at them, and they joined the head of the parade, just behind Mary Gibbons and The New Kid. Mary and The New Kid were carrying a big banner that said:

HELP SAVE OUR ENVIRONMENT!
DON'T LITTER.

"Here we go," Alvin said in a low voice. In one hand he carried a paper sack that looked like it was full of trash.

"Here we go," echoed the Pest. "Oh, Alvin, it's so exciting!" She was carrying an immense wad of crumpled wastepaper which she somehow had tied into a gigantic ball with a long piece of string. The ball towered high above her head so she couldn't

see, and she blundered blindly down the street wandering from curb to curb.

Shoie had an old tire over each shoulder. And, wound several times around his wrist was a long electrical cord. The cord obviously was not trash.

"Hey, Shoie! Watcha c-c-c-c-carrying the c-c-c-wire for?" asked Worm Wormley.

"You'll see!" shouted Shoie. "Take a look around."

Sure enough, several of the other kids had long extension cords looped around their waists or across their shoulders.

By now, porch lights were flashing on all along Main Street, and adults were streaming out of their houses to watch the procession. As soon as they read the sign at the head of the column, they started clapping and cheering the kids on.

Meanwhile the column was growing steadily in size as it was joined, not only by other kids who were in on the plan, but also by little kids, big kids, dogs, cats, even adults. And the adults who didn't join the parade began walking beside it down the sidewalk to find out what was going to happen next.

To Alvin it was an exciting sight, and he gloried in the swell of sound. Superweasel had planned the whole thing. Right under the noses of the adults, Superweasel had inspired the kids to clean up the entire town of Riverton.

There was no way that traffic could move down Main Street, so drivers abandoned their cars and joined the parade, swelling its already swollen ranks.

Old Mr. Grunnion came barreling down his driveway in his motorized wheelchair, waving one arm and shouting the kids on. Shoie made a place for him at the head of the column. The girl marching beside Shoie discovered that she had overestimated her strength, and now was staggering under a load of plastic bags filled with tin cans that was simply too big for her. Old Mr. Grunnion grabbed one of the bags, balanced it on his lap, shouted "Charge!" and turned up his wheelchair to full speed ahead.

Gary Hines had been taking care of his little niece Melissa, who was one and a half years old. He wasn't supposed to leave the house, but he couldn't resist. He piled her into his old wagon and joined the parade. She was so entranced with all the noise and movement that at the corner of Maple and Main Streets she fell out of the wagon. Gary, his eyes shining with excitement, didn't miss her for almost four blocks. Fortunately a Madison schoolboy saw her fall, snatched her up, and dropped her into the bushel basket of soggy newspapers he was carrying.

At the corner of Oak Street, Miss Miles, who really had started the whole thing by assigning her students a pollution project, joined the head of the column. She looked across at Alvin. There was a proud smile on her face.

Wouldn't she be surprised, thought Alvin, *if she knew I was Superweasel?*

But the thought was swept from his mind as the head of the column came to the end of Main Street and rolled irresistibly across the square toward City Hall. The building, built of white stone, was gleaming in the floodlights that were turned on each night.

As he crossed the street Alvin looked to his left, then his right, and saw two equally big parades of kids—and adults—marching from those directions. And he knew that still another column was approaching the back of the building.

"Come on!" he shouted.

He, Shoie and the Pest raced on ahead, and were joined on the sidewalk that approached the City Hall steps by the four kids from the other schools, who had organized the parades. Each of these kids was carrying not trash, but supplies. Within seconds they had driven stakes into the ground on each side of the walk, and attached signs to them. The sign pointing to the left said METAL AND GLASS; the sign to the right said PAPER, WOOD, AND CLOTH.

The signs went up just in time. By now the whole city square was packed with people, and the columns came to an abrupt halt. Then the kids came forward, at first one-by-one, then in groups, and dumped the trash that had so recently littered every street, every yard, and every alley of Riverton. Soft materials to the right, which could be sold for reprocessing, and solid materials to the left, which presented more of an environmental problem.

But Superweasel had already thought out one solution. They could sell the cans and bottles if they could reduce them to a manageable form.

"Quick!" Alvin said to Shoie. "Take charge of the extension cords."

Shoie dashed over to the City Hall steps, where a dozen other kids were already waiting, each with an extension cord in his hands. He waved for a couple of the kids to follow him, and slipped inside the door. Within thirty seconds they reappeared, unrolling three electric cords down the steps. When they came to the end of their cords, other boys plugged in and continued. Soon they had three outlets by the big piles of bottles and cans.

As if from nowhere three boys appeared on the lawn. Two were pulling garden carts, the third a homemade wagon. All three carried identical, if strange, loads.

"What are those, Alvin?" shouted Irma Watney, her eyes glowing.

"Trash smashers!" he shouted back.

It had been the knottiest problem of all. The "organizing committee" had chosen Theresa Undermine to solve the problem because she had a reputation as the most persuasive speaker in Roosevelt School.

Theresa had cornered Mr. Bilzer in the office of his appliance store. Fifteen minutes later she had emerged with a victorious smile—and with the loan of three trash compactors. Mr. Bilzer also emerged, but with a slightly dazed expression. Theresa had guaranteed that she would demonstrate the trash compactors to *hundreds* if not *thousands* of potential customers.

Now willing hands quickly unloaded the appliances

onto the lawn, and plugged them into the extension cords that snaked out of City Hall.

Theresa pulled out a large drawer, loaded in a heavy paper bag, and motioned to Shoie to fill it with old bottles. When it was full, she pushed it back in its cabinet and pressed a button. There was a soft whirrrr and a grinding sound. When she pulled out the drawer again, all the bottles had been smashed into a thin layer in the bottom. Several times she and Shoie did this. Then Shoie (the muscleman) lifted the bag from the drawer. Inside was a heavy block of smashed glass. Soon all three trash compactors were in operation and the pile of blocks, some filled with glass and some filled with flattened cans, grew rapidly.

The city square by now was an incredible sight. Alvin knew that Riverton had been littered, but he had no idea that a total clean-up would uncover so much junk.

The kids had started a third pile of trash—items too big to put in the other two piles: old mattresses and springs, doors and window frames, tree limbs, the entire roof of a shed, car fenders and radiators, even a badly cracked set of concrete steps. Alvin had no idea how the kids had managed to move the steps, but by now he was convinced that, if they tried hard enough, they could do almost anything. As he watched, the kids heaved the old Volkswagen onto the stack. Inside, the little boy was still peering through his thick glasses at the shattered windshield. Shoie hauled him out over violent protests.

As the kids finished dumping their loads they retreated across the street to join the adults on the sidewalk. When the sidewalk too was jammed, they overflowed onto the street itself.

The trash mashers were operating full blast, stamping out blocks of trash like they were building blocks. Worm Wormley and Shoie formed the blocks into a long line, then placed other blocks on top. Soon they had a wall at least twelve feet long and six feet high.

The Pest slipped through the crowd and crossed the street to Lunt's Hardware Store. Sure enough, Mr. Lunt was inside, cheering the kids on between puffs of his pipe. When the Pest knocked on his door, he let her in. Two minutes later she was back, tugging at Alvin's sleeve.

"Look what I've got." In her hand she held a can of bright orange spray paint. "I thought we'd paint a sign on that wall they're building."

He thought for a moment, then whispered to her.

The Pest skipped over to the growing wall. She looked at it thoughtfully. Then, reaching up as high as she could, she started spraying her sign.

When it was finished, the crowd shouted its appreciation. The sign said: DONATED TO THE CITY BY SUPERWEASEL AND THE KIDS OF RIVERTON.

Alvin glanced around. His eyes happened to meet those of Miss Miles. She was looking thoughtfully at him. He turned and sauntered up the steps of City Hall, trying to look innocent. Under his arm he still carried the paper sack.

It was time for Superweasel's final adventure.

17. Superweasel's Final Adventure

There was virtually no activity inside City Hall. Alvin could hear only the crackle of the radio in the Police Department as he crept past the door, and the scrape of the duty sergeant's chair at his desk.

He came to the bottom of a broad stairway and started up. At the second floor he paused, but everything seemed clear. He headed on up to the top floor. He had worn his sneakers, and made no sound as he walked carefully down the third floor hallway. He stopped in front of a phone booth. Slipping inside, he pushed the door shut behind him. Instantly the overhead light came on, so he reached up and unscrewed the bulb. Even in the phone booth he could hear the shouts of the crowd outdoors but there didn't seem to be anyone on the third floor.

Alvin slipped quietly into the costume, and pulled the mask down over his face. For a fleeting moment he wished there was a mirror in the phone booth so he could take one final look at Superweasel; *after tonight,* he thought, *Superweasel will vanish into the great afterworld where Superman, Batman and all those other superheroes of yesterday now reside.* The thought made him a little sad.

He eased out of the phone booth and headed for the door at the end of the corridor. It was marked Emergency Use Only, and Alvin knew that it led out onto a fire escape that angled down the front of the City Hall. He'd inspected the City Hall from top to bottom when his class had studied city government.

His heart was pounding now. Although he'd had more than his share of adventures for a boy of his age, he knew that this could be the turning point of his life. Would he be greeted as a criminal—or as a superhero?

Alvin planned to step out onto the fire escape high above the heads of the crowd. He had confidence that, as soon as the kids saw him, they'd start cheering. Hadn't Superweasel organized all of them to perform this mighty feat? And when the kids started cheering, maybe their parents would forget the vandalism, and start cheering, too. Then Alvin—Superweasel—would modestly hold up his hands for silence, just as he'd seen the president do on television. The cheering and applause would go on for a while, of course, but gradually it would die down. At just the proper moment Superweasel would begin his speech.

He'd practiced that speech in his mind a hundred times, and had even whispered it once before the mirror in his room. He'd tell the truth and nothing else. How he—and his sister and Shoie—had invented Superweasel in order to help fight pollution; the horrible stinking mess they'd found where the Weasel

River ran past the chemical plant, and how they'd succeeded in changing all that; how he'd bravely and heroically climbed to the top of the foundry chimney. (*Oops!*, he said to himself. *Better leave out "bravely" and "heroically" if you're going to tell nothing but the truth. Instead, tell them how scared you were. Then they'll sympathize with you.*)

And he *did* need their sympathy—the sympathy of everyone in town. For he planned to tell them exactly what else had happened. How another Superweasel had popped up in town, and how this one had become a vandal instead of a superhero.

Indeed this could be the turning point of his life.

He stood as straight and tall as he could. He lifted his head. Superweasel placed his hand on the doorknob. He was ready to face the world.

As he turned the doorknob he heard the swelling roar of the crowd, suddenly excited. There were cheers and whistles from the kids, and shouts of anger from the adults gathered below on the city square.

Confused, Alvin wondered, dimly, how they could have seen him through the door. Had they known in advance that he would appear? Well, at least they were there, waiting for him.

He pushed open the door, and stepped out onto the grillwork that formed the third-floor landing of the fire escape.

Instantly the cheers stopped. Alvin wondered why. For a few seconds he was blinded by the bright lights that flooded City Hall. There was no sound from the vast crowd below.

Alvin took a step forward to the railing of the fire escape and held up his two arms to command silence. It was a useless gesture, for already there was total silence. The soundless night finally was shattered by a shrill voice saying clearly, "Look, mommy! There's two of them!"

By now his eyes were adapting to the light, and Alvin could make out the upturned faces below. For a moment the meaning of the child's words escaped him. He lowered his arms and gripped the railing. It was time to make his speech.

At that moment he heard a furtive movement behind him, toward the corner of the fire-escape landing. Alvin whirled.

There, crouched against the wall, was—*Superweasel!*

The two costumed figures confronted each other for what seemed an eternity. A dozen thoughts tumbled through Alvin's mind. Here at last was the impostor. But *who* was it? How could anyone else tell who was the *real* Superweasel? *Who* would be hauled into court as the vandal?

"Stop! Stay where you are, both of you! You're under arrest!" The commanding voice of Officer Twilley came up from below. Alvin felt the steel stairway vibrate slightly, and knew that the police officer was on his way up to capture them.

Alvin glanced around at the imposter. At that very moment the figure raced up the stairway toward the roof.

Alvin leaped up the stairway after the imposter.

As he dashed up the steps Alvin could see the crowd through the grillwork at his feet. The sight of all those upturned faces made him dizzy, and he stumbled on one of the steps, painfully skinning his shin. He fell to his knees, grabbing for the railing.

The fire escape was shaking more violently now, and he knew that Officer Twilley was gaining steadily. Alvin struggled to his feet and looked up the stairway just in time to see the impostor vanish over the edge of the roof. The sight gave Alvin a new burst of energy—he *couldn't* let that guy out of his sight. He raced up the stairway and threw himself over the low wall that circled the roof.

It was much darker on top of the building, but Alvin could see the dim figure running along the edge. Alvin sprinted after him. Suddenly the figure vanished. For a moment Alvin thought he had tumbled over the low wall, but then he heard a loud "Oooof!" The impostor obviously had tripped over one of the vents that projected up through the roofing.

Alvin pounced on the figure and hauled him to his feet. Even in the dim light, it was the best view he'd had of the impostor, who was a bit taller than himself, and somewhat heavier. Otherwise, it seemed to Alvin that he was looking at his twin. Same cape, same shirt, same grinning animal mask.

Alvin Fernald took charge. "Do you want to escape?" he asked urgently.

The impostor instantly nodded his head.

"Then follow me!"

Alvin knew there was a little concrete-block building perched on top of the roof; it held the ventilating equipment. He could think of nowhere else to hide, even though it would only delay discovery. Officer Twilley's head would appear over the railing at any moment.

Alvin fled across the dim roof and snatched open the door of the little building. The impostor was right on his heels. Together they slammed the door shut and leaned against it. Alvin looked around.

There was only one window in the structure, but it let in a feeble glow from the starlit sky. Directly in front of Alvin was a huge fan, and just beyond it was a yawning black hole at least three feet in diameter. He stepped around the fan and peered into the blackness. He could see nothing. Cautiously he slid out his foot. The flooring continued beneath it, but it seemed to bend slightly as he put his weight on that leg. He reached both arms into the yawning black hole, and could feel smooth, curving surfaces on each side. Apparently he was standing in the opening of a huge sheetmetal ventilating duct that ran down into the building.

The Magnificent Brain took over momentarily. Why not lie down in the darkness of the duct just behind the fan? There was a slim chance that the police, in searching the little structure, might overlook them.

Alvin lay down on his stomach and pulled the other figure down beside him. Footsteps approached the door.

Without realizing what he was doing, Alvin scrunched farther back into the duct. Immediately the cold metal floor gave way beneath him, and he started to slide. Frantically he grasped the cape of the figure beside him. Then both figures were swooping and sliding down into the blackness.

Alvin's fingernails clawed at the smooth metal and found absolutely nothing to hang onto. As the duct slanted down it seemed to get steeper and steeper. The two figures picked up speed in the pitch blackness, and soon were hurtling, one after the other, toward—who knew what?

BLANNNNNGGGG!

Alvin's feet smashed into something, smashed into it so hard that it gave way with a resounding noise. At the same moment the ducting gave way beneath his stomach and he felt himself flying through space.

THUDDDD!

His feet hit the floor, and instinctively he bent his knees to cushion his fall.

OOOOOOFFFFF!

The second figure tumbled to the floor beside him.

Both boys were dazed. Alvin waggled his head, then looked around. Across the room a door was open, and there was an overhead bulb burning in the corridor outside; light spilled through the doorway and into the room.

Alvin immediately knew where he was. He was lying on the thick carpeting of the City Council meeting room. Turning, he glanced up at the wall above his head. Sure enough, there was a gaping hole. They had slid down the big ventilating shaft, knocked out the cover of the duct, and tumbled into the City Council's chambers.

Alvin listened intently. There were muffled shouts from above, then a clear voice coming down the ventilating shaft, "They aren't on the roof or in the ventilating shed. They've vanished. I don't know how they did it. They've vanished into thin air!"

Alvin looked at the impostor. "Are you hurt?" he whispered.

"No," the figure gasped. "Just knocked my wind out." There was something about the voice that was strangely familiar.

"Come on. I know a way out of here through the service entrance. If we're lucky we won't get caught."

18. Unmasked!

Two Superweasels crept down the alley between Maple and Third Streets. When they came to York Avenue, with its bright streetlights, they hung back in the shadow of Mr. Lempke's garage.

"I'll lead the way," Alvin whispered. "When we're sure no one is around, we'll sneak across the street. The park is only one block away. We'll head for it. Then we'll climb down the bank of the river, and work our way upstream. I think we can make it out of town, now that we got this far away from City Hall without being captured."

"I hope so. We had a narrow escape back there." A pause. Then, "Thanks for helping me."

Again Alvin had the feeling that he knew who was behind the mask—but he just couldn't place the voice.

A rather strange thought passed through his mind. After the dangers they'd been through together in the past half-hour, he'd begun to *like* the other Superweasel. He had to force himself to remember that whoever was behind that mask had broken windows and slashed tires, then tried to put the blame on him. Nobody was perfect, though. . . .

Alvin suddenly remembered the time long ago when, on a dare, he'd stolen a handful of nails from Lunt's Hardware Store; and the time he'd intentionally stepped on the Pest's new dancing shoes (and scuffed them beyond repair) because she was the center of attention. Shame rose up in his throat. He supposed that everyone did things they were ashamed of, now and then.

As though he were a mind reader, the boy behind the mask reached out and touched him on the shoulder. "Thanks," he said again. "Thanks for everything. I mean, thanks for helping me get away from the police, and thanks for not clobbering me, especially after I caused you so much trouble by making everybody blame you for—" His voice trailed off. Shame had closed *his* throat, too.

"Come on, let's go." Alvin tried to make his voice harsh. "We're still not safe in these outfits, and we don't have time to get out of them here."

He scurried across the bright street and ran headlong through a backyard to reach the fence that ran around the park. It was a low fence, and he was across it within seconds, then fleeing toward the river. In the darkness he slipped down the bank, and almost fell into the water. Another figure slid down to join him.

"Who's there?" The voice belonged to Mr. Figgens, who took care of the park.

"Come on!" Alvin whispered urgently. He floundered upstream, half in and half out of the water.

Hours seemed to pass as he pushed himself to his physical limit, the other Superweasel matching him stride for stride. Occasionally they thought they heard pursuers, and stopped to listen. Once, when they were far out of town, they heard startled voices from a car parked right on the bank of the river. Still they splashed on upstream.

As he worked his way around a bend, it occurred to Alvin that by now he must be covered with mud—and that the mud no longer smelled the way it did when he, Shoie and the Pest had worked their way up the river. It seemed a very long time ago that Superweasel had set out to cure the world's pollution. *Well,* he thought, *at least we did some good. We cleaned up Weasel River.*

He sniffed, and smelled nothing but the sharply sweet smell of the newly budded trees that rose on either side of the stream. *It may be quite a while before we catch any fish in Three Oaks Pond,* he thought, *but Superweasel really did clean up the river—and stopped the smoke from the foundry and organized all the kids to clean up Riverton like it's never been cleaned up before.*

He was mentally patting himself on the back for a job well done when he floundered around another bend and spotted bright lights ahead. They were approaching the chemical plant. In fact, just a few yards farther Alvin stumbled across what remained of the dam he and Shoie had built. He scrambled up and sat astride the drain pipe from the factory. For some time now he had heard no signs of pursuit.

"I think we're safe now," he said to the figure that stumbled through the water toward him. "Let's stop and rest. We'll get rid of these outfits, and head back to town from another direction. I don't think anybody knows who we are."

A moment of silence. Then, "I know who you are, Alvin."

Alvin was taken by surprise. So Superweasel was not really a mystery figure after all! Again there was that nagging familiarity of the voice. . . .

"If you know who I am," he said, "there's no reason to keep my face covered." He ripped off the mask and threw it onto the bank. He stared at the other figure. The floodlights from the chemical plant clearly illuminated the mask. Who was behind it?

"Who are you?" Alvin asked.

"I'm too ashamed to show you."

"If you really are ashamed of what you've done, then down deep you must be a pretty good guy," said Alvin. It was a very profound thought, and he felt like an adult as soon as he said it. He also felt better about stealing the nails, and deliberately ruining his sister's shoes.

"I can never make everything right again."

"You can try. But the first thing to do is take off the mask."

Hesitantly, one arm reached up to the chin of the

mask. Then in one swift movement the mask was swept off and sailed through the air, to land on the bank beside Alvin's mask.

There, in front of Alvin, stood Windy Biggs.

Alvin was surprised, then sensed exactly what had happened, even before the words came tumbling from Windy's lips.

"It all started when you deliberately pushed me into the river on the way home from school that day. At least I thought you did it on purpose. Did you?"

"Cross my heart I didn't. I was fooling around, which I shouldn't have been doing, but I slipped and couldn't avoid hitting you. Cross my heart."

"Anyway, I *thought* you did it on purpose. And I swore I'd get even with you. Then, after you'd sneaked into the chemical plant, my father showed me the bucket you left behind. I recognized it right away. It has a yellow 'F' painted on it. I suppose that stands for 'Fernald.' Once last fall I saw your little sister wearing it for a football helmet. Suddenly I knew you were Superweasel. Later, I asked my father if the plant really *was* polluting the river, and he said no. He said it several times, very loud. I believed him. I really did. Wouldn't you believe anything your father told you?"

"Yes. Yes, I suppose I would," said Alvin, thinking of his own father. He didn't say it, but he thought how awful it would be to find out that Dad really was lying, *deliberately* lying, to him.

"That made me even more determined to get even with you, and when your picture appeared in the paper, dressed as Superweasel, I saw my chance. I made a costume that looked just as much like yours as I possibly could. I even bought a mask like yours at the Nifty Novelty Shop. Then, to get even, I did all those awful things—broke windows, ruined tires, sprayed paint all over—so Superweasel would get the blame."

There was a pause. Then Windy continued in a low voice: "When I found out my father was lying—about polluting the river—you'd think I'd have been sorry. But I wasn't. That just made me madder, because you had shown him up for what he is—a liar. Next week I was going to break some more windows. Then I was going to write a letter to the police and tell them that Alvin Fernald was Superweasel. I figured they'd find your costume somewhere around your house, and then you'd really be in trouble."

Silence, except for the river gurgling at their feet. Then, "You may not believe what I'm going to say, Alvin, but it really is the truth. I changed my mind. I suddenly realized that I hated doing those awful things, even though I did them. Then I got in a big argument with my father, about the pollution, and about his lies. He began shouting at me. He said it was none of my business what happened at the chemical plant. I said it was everybody's business. I-I-well, I began to cry for the first time in three or four years, Alvin. I ran to my room. Later that night, I came up the river, up to here. By then, of course, thanks to you and the newspaper articles, my father had been forced to stop polluting the water."

Windy waved his hand at the water trickling along beneath their feet. "I took your dam apart. The water smells good out here now."

Another silence.

"What were you doing on the fire escape, Windy?"

"I'd made up my mind to tell everyone what I'd done. I was going to do it tonight, from the fire escape, where everybody could hear me. And I'm still going to do it. I'm going to pay for all that damage I did." Windy took a couple of steps along the stream bed, then stood motionless. "I don't mean that my *father* will pay for it. That wouldn't mean anything. I'll pay for it, with money I earn myself, *even if it takes a hundred thousand years!*"

What a mess, thought Alvin. *And all because I accidentally pushed him in the river, and his father told a lie.* In a way, Windy was only partially to blame for what had happened. And he certainly had learned his lesson.

Alvin cleared his throat. "I really don't think it will take that long, Windy. I'll help you find some summer jobs. Shoie and my sister will help, too. With all of us scouting around, I'll bet we can find you so many jobs that you'll have the damage all paid for by the middle of the summer." He grew more enthusiastic. "Yep. We'll repay every penny. Then Superweasel can vanish with a clear conscience!"

"But Superweasel isn't going to just vanish. At least this one isn't. I'm going to tell Mr. Moser that I'm the one who did all the damage. He'll put it in the paper. Then everyone will know."

"Let's think about that for just a minute, Windy. I suppose you're right. You'll never feel right until you admit that you're the vandal. But if you announce it *right now*, then everybody who had any damage will go to your father for payment. And he'll pay off." Alvin looked sympathetically at the other boy. "It isn't your fault your old man is rich, Windy. But he *is* rich. And he'll try to use his money to help you out."

"You're right. He'll punish me, but he'll insist on paying for all the damage."

"Okay. Then the only thing to do is to keep your identity secret until after you've paid off every penny. *Then* you can go to Mr. Moser and tell him everything."

After a long silence, Windy said, "I suppose you're right. I really want to pay for that damage all by myself, Alvin."

Alvin looked straight at Windy. He held out his fist, thumb sticking straight up. "Grab my thumb, and then stick up your own thumb, Windy."

Perplexed, Windy did as he was told.

"Power to Superweasel!" intoned Alvin.

"Power to Superweasel!" Windy's voice dropped to a hoarse whisper. "And thanks to Superweasel, too."

"Come on, Windy," Alvin said. "It's time to bury Superweasel forever."

They struggled out of their costumes. Alvin found a large rock beside the stream and, pushing together, they managed to tip it on its side. In the hollow beneath the rock they laid the two costumes. For a moment they both looked down. The two masks grinned up at them. Then, without another word, they tipped the big rock back into place.

Superweasel was gone forever, joining all the other legendary superheroes.

19. A Grade for Superweasel

It had taken a century and a half for Riverton to accumulate all that junk, from horseshoe nails and old plow handles to TV sets and electric toothbrushes. It's not surprising, therefore, that it took the town's two garbage trucks more than three days just to cart the stuff away from City Hall and properly dispose of it.

Suddenly the citizens of Riverton had an intense new pride in their town. Vacant lots that once had been neighborhood dumps now revealed, for the first time in decades, the budding beauty of spring vegetation. Streets and alleys were clean. A week before, almost any resident would have flipped an empty cigarette pack or candy-bar wrapper into the gutter. Now the mere fact that the gutter was clean made him pause, then stuff the wastepaper into his pocket. And if he *did* toss it into the gutter, some other citizen was likely to remind him, gently but firmly, that Riverton was the cleanest town in America. And it must be kept that way.

Other things happened, too, like ripples going out

from a stone tossed into Three Oaks Pond. The story of the kids' sensational clean-up campaign reached the Governor's ears, and he made a special visit to Riverton to declare it the state's Model City of the Year. Mayor Bienfang, giving the kids full credit, stated: "Other politicians may question the behavior of today's youth, but not once have I lost faith in the children of Riverton."

The City Council voted funds for one hundred sparkling new trash cans to be placed throughout the city. (It also voted funds to repair some mysterious but minor damage to the City Council's chambers.)

The Elks Club, in cooperation with the Riverton Boy Scouts, organized a recycling center where citizens could turn in their wastepaper, bottles and cans for resale to manufacturers, thus preserving natural resources while keeping the town litter-free.

Mr. Bilzer sold eighteen trash compactors in one week, and tried to hire Theresa Undermine as a permanent salesgirl.

Mayor Bienfang was so carried away that, for the fourth time, he applied to the federal government for funds to help build a new sewage treatment plant; the city had outgrown the capacity of the existing one. This time, however, he bravely addressed the application directly to the president, and enclosed some newspaper clippings. The request was promptly granted.

The owner of the gas station at the corner of Main and York offered a free analysis of any car's exhaust to find out whether the car was a dangerous polluter.

Windy Biggs's father, having felt the heat of bad publicity, announced that the Biggs Chemical Company was contributing $5,000 toward the stocking of Three Oaks Pond "so Riverton children can once more have the age-old fun of catching fish." Fingerlings were promptly turned loose in the pond by the thousands.

Finally, Old Grandpa Hein, who had been hard of hearing for twenty-five years, announced in a letter to the editor that noise, too, was a form of environmental pollution; that people shouldn't disturb other people by shouting; and that he therefore (at long last) was buying a hearing aid.

More intriguing to the citizens, though, was speculation as to the identity of Superweasel—or rather, *two* Superweasels. Virtually the entire town had seen the drama unfold on the fire escape that night. Furthermore, the disappearance into thin air of the two identical figures was not just baffling—it was incredible.

In a column for the *Daily Bugle* Mr. Moser pointed out that a Superweasel impostor apparently had committed the acts of vandalism; and that the real Superweasel, thanks to his fight against pollution, had made Riverton a considerably cleaner city. "Our hearts and thoughts go out to that masked figure, wherever he may be, in his unceasing battle to clean up our planet."

And in that same issue of the *Daily Bugle*, just beside Mr. Moser's column, appeared a letter that made the citizens of Riverton even more curious about the two Superweasels who had so mysteriously vanished:

144

To the Editor:

I, Superweasel Number Two, am entirely to blame for all the recent acts of vandalism. The *real* Superweasel had nothing to do with them.

To make amends for that damage, I am asking Mr. Al Moser of the *Daily Bugle* to supervise a special "Superweasel Fund." Anyone who suffered loss through my destructive acts should promptly let Mr. Moser know how much money it will take to pay in full for the damage. Over the next several weeks I will send Mr. Moser money which I have earned—money which will enable him to pay these bills. Finally the slate will be clean.

As soon as the last penny is paid, I will reveal my identity as the imitation Superweasel.

And I hope, at that time, that the real Superweasel also will unmask himself, for we owe him a great deal. Riverton is a far better town because of his mysterious visits to fight pollution.

(Signed) Superweasel Number Two

Alvin had dreaded this moment for weeks. Shoie and Windy had dreaded it, too. It came during the final week of school.

Most of the kids had already given reports on their antipollution projects.

Now Miss Miles nodded at Windy. "Oliver, you may now report on your environmental work."

"Uh, I'm afraid I didn't do much to help the environment, Miss Miles."

"But Oliver. I thought you were distributing litera-

145

ture to housewives about harmful chemicals in their detergents."

"Uh, yes, Miss Miles, I guess I did a little of that. But not very much." He lifted his head and looked directly at her. "I don't really deserve a passing grade."

The class gasped.

"Ummmm. Well, at least you are honest about it." She nodded at Shoie. "And you, Wilfred?"

There was an agonizing silence. Then Shoie said in a low voice, "Alvin and I planned something, but it didn't turn out the way we planned."

"At least you can share your plans with the class." Another pause. "No I can't."

"Why not, Wilfred?"

"Just can't."

"And you, Alvin?"

Alvin struggled up straight in his seat. "Like Shoie says." He crossed his legs and picked at the worn spot on the heel of his right sneaker.

"Is that all you have to say?"

"Yes. Except Shoie and Windy and I helped clean up the litter and take it to City Hall."

"I hope you're telling the truth, Alvin. I saw you arrive there with nothing but a paper sack."

"Well—" Alvin's mind was a blank. "Well, I got rid of what was in the paper sack." Then, more thoughtfully, "Yep, I sure did get rid of what was in that sack."

The bell rang. Kids shuffled to their feet. Papers and books disappeared into desks.

"I've given each of you a grade on your antipollution project, along with some comments," said Miss

146

Miles, her voice rising above the din. "You can pick up your grades on the way out. Alvin, Wilfred and Oliver—I want to see you for a few minutes after school.

The three boys waited in agony while the rest of the kids picked up their grades. Theresa Undermine squealed in mock surprise at the "A" on her sheet of paper, even though Theresa always got "A" in everything. Worm Wormley was proud of his "B-."

Finally all the other kids were gone, and silence fell across the classroom. Alvin squirmed at his desk.

Miss Miles, seated behind her desk, looked up at the three boys. "I asked you to stay," she said brightly, "because I didn't want the rest of the class to know the grades that I am giving you for your antipollution projects. I didn't think you'd *want* those grades known." She held up three slips of paper.

Here comes the bad news, thought Alvin. *We've flunked.* He and the other two boys approached her desk.

There was a very large "A" on Alvin's paper. Just beneath, in Miss Miles' neat handwriting, appeared the sentence, "Thanks for a wonderful antipollution project, which took a great deal of imagination."

Alvin was astounded. He glanced across at Shoie's paper. It was identical to his.

He looked up at Miss Miles. Her eyes were shining brightly and there was a proud smile on her face.

Alvin stared at her. Finally a thought flashed through the old M.B., and a smile flickered across his face, too. "Then you know our secret?" he asked.

"What secret?" she said innocently. "All I know is what I observe."

She turned and picked up a piece of chalk. Across the blackboard she wrote, "Who knows what vengeance Superweasel will take against defilers of our planet? Beware, polluters! Someday Superweasel may strike again!"

Miss Miles carefully replaced the chalk and turned around, the smile still on her face, a twinkle in her eye.

She turned to Windy. "I had to give you an 'Incomplete' on your project, Oliver, for reasons I think you can readily understand. However, I imagine you'll complete your project sometime this summer." She paused. "Incidentally, Mr. Moser has offered to keep me posted on the Superweasel Fund. I imagine you'll complete your project just about the time that Mr. Moser pays for the damage that some unknown person did."

Windy was gazing at the floor.

"Okay, kids. See you tomorrow. Last day of school."

It was the first time she had ever called them kids. It was a fine sign.

It was a fine day, too. The boys sailed down the school steps in a single bound, and ran down Maple Street together. The early summer sun felt comfortably hot on Alvin's back. He reached inside his pocket and pulled out a package of gum.

Up ahead he could see a crow circling an incredibly blue sky. How great it would be to have the freedom of a crow. . . . He handed Shoie and Windy each a stick of gum. Then he flapped his arms once, held them straight out, and soared across the street. The other two flapped along behind.

"Let's go out to Three Oaks Pond," Alvin said, catching his breath. "Maybe we can spot some of those fish they turned loose."

The three boys headed down Maple Street. Absently, Alvin squeezed the gum wrapper into a ball, and dropped it in the gutter.

Instantly both Shoie and Windy broke stride, and stooped over to pick up the wrapper. Their heads bonked together, and they staggered off in opposite directions.

A small voice piped up from just behind them:

> *Little Bo-Peep*
> *Has found a heap*
> *Of refuse in the gutter;*
> *She stuffs it in*
> *The corner bin*
> *"Right on!" shouts her mutter.*

" 'Mutter?' " groaned Shoie, holding his forehead.

"Sure. You know. Like your mom. Mutter."

The little figure tagged along after the three boys. Alvin Fernald, ex-Superweasel, led the way toward the cold, clear waters of Three Oaks Pond.

ABOUT THE AUTHOR

Clifford B. Hicks was born and raised in a town in Iowa much like Riverton, the scene of *Alvin Fernald, Superweasel*. He began writing professionally during his high school years, when he was a correspondent for the Des Moines *Register and Tribune*. He is now special projects editor of a scientific and mechanical trade magazine in Chicago.

A graduate of Northwestern University, Mr. Hicks spends his leisure time with his woodworking, his writing, and his three sons, who are, he says, his severest critics.

Mr. Hicks is the author of four other Alvin Fernald adventures: *The Marvelous Inventions of Alvin Fernald, Alvin's Secret Code, Alvin Fernald, Foreign Trader,* and *Alvin Fernald: Mayor for a Day*.

Alvin Fernald will be seen on television for the first time in 1974, on "The Wonderful World of Walt Disney."